6-30-15

God Made
The Rainbow

a love story

KEN REGAN

WestBow Press books may be ordered through booksellers or by contacting:

WestBow Press
A Division of Thomas Nelson & Zondervan
1663 Liberty Drive
Bloomington, IN 47403
www.westbowpress.com
1 (866) 928-1240

ISBN: 978-1-4908-7312-1 (sc)
ISBN: 978-1-4908-7313-8 (hc)
ISBN: 978-1-4908-7311-4 (e)

Library of Congress Control Number: 2015903963

Print information available on the last page.

WestBow Press rev. date: 03/10/2015

to Christine - the real life (and still very much alive) Jenny
and to Chris & Alicia and Heather & Joe –
great parents to my grandchildren

Note to the reader: If you've read my previous book, *A Christmas Miracle Comes to Holy Nativity*, you may find that a couple of scenes in this book bear some similarity to scenes in *A Christmas Miracle*. Here's the reason why: those scenes were actually written for this book first. I set this book aside for a time to begin work on *A Christmas Miracle* and found myself drawing upon certain scenes from *God Made the Rainbow*. When I came back to this work, I contemplated changing those scenes (and did to some degree), but in the end I found that they were too important to alter drastically or leave out altogether. This is because those particular scenes came the closest to the real life way I met my future wife and her two children, which had a heavy influence on the stories I have tried to tell. So please excuse the self-plagiarism (you can always make a game out of it – spot the similarities). And if you haven't read *A Christmas Miracle*, I can only ask, "Why not?"

PROLOGUE

"**O**w! For the love of ..."

He pressed his thumb against his left forefinger and watched the drops of blood ooze out. It was a minor injury. The knife did not cut deeply. He rinsed his finger under the kitchen faucet.

He was not a cook, he thought to himself. He was useless around the kitchen. At least now he had learned that it was probably better to prepare a salad by tearing the lettuce apart with his hands rather than trying to cut it with a sharp knife.

Becky and Lisa would be down soon looking for dinner. They probably also still harbored hopes of seeing their mother, not Michael, at the kitchen counter preparing the meal. But Jenny was dead. The truth had to sink in eventually. It was time for the girls to get used to their stepfather being both a mother and a father to them. But it was not something Michael himself was used to yet. Jenny was gone, leaving her two young daughters in his care.

This was not going to be an easy dinner, regardless of Michael's cooking abilities, or lack thereof. It would be their first time together since the funeral. Michael's thoughts kept taking him back to the minister's words at the grave site.

"There is sadness over the loss of Jennifer Farley Griggs. But we need not be sad for her. She is happy now and in a better place."

The words were hollow. Michael stared into the minister's face and wondered if this were some stock sermon that he used at all funerals. To think, he came so close to being like this minister. It could have been him standing in that place delivering the same words. Could he have done it? Would it have been as meaningless for him as it obviously was for this gray haired, overweight minister? Michael looked at his two stepdaughters standing next to his sister Julie, tears on Becky's face and confusion in Lisa's. How could this man say not to be sad for Jenny? She was taken away from her two little girls. She was only 27 years old. She had her whole life before her. She had a new husband. They were going to make a life together, be a family. But the cancer took it all away.

The cancer even took Michael's faith away. The years of seminary were wasted. They were married right after his graduation, two weeks before Michael accepted his first call. But he decided to turn down the call when the tumor was discovered less than a month after their wedding day. He wanted to devote all his energies to her, to spend every moment with her.

The minister began to speak of God's grace. Michael found himself stifling a laugh of disgust. Where was the grace in such a cruel death? What kind of God would play such a cosmic trick? There were times when Jenny was very ill that Michael was angry at God. He wasn't angry any longer. Now he felt nothing. He had no sense of there being anything in existence out there to be angry at. He had lost his faith. He couldn't in good conscience follow the path of ordained ministry. He asked to quit. His Bishop talked him into going on leave from call instead until he could seek pastoral guidance and straighten his feelings out. But he never went to any of the counseling sessions set up for him.

As they sat at the kitchen table, Michael's feelings were all over the place. He stole awkward glances at these girls sitting on either side of him. Nine-year-old Becky on his left, her short dark hair was nothing like her mother's. But her eyes were. Every time Michael looked at her, he saw Jenny's eyes staring back at him. Michael was afraid to return her piercing gaze. He focused more of his attention on Lisa. Her dusty brown hair falling at her shoulders was just like Jenny's. She had her mother's smile too. Michael watched as she happily fumbled with the overcooked spaghetti he had prepared. Only six years old, far too young to be without a mother. They were both so young. And Michael was too young to be shouldering such a responsibility. He was only 25, just out of school for the first time since kindergarten. He should have been basking in new found independence. Instead, he found himself the head of a family. How in the world did Jenny ever manage to be responsible for a tiny baby while barely 18 herself?

"So, how's the spaghetti?" he asked, nervously, to break the silence. He felt like he wanted to talk to them about Jenny, but he didn't know what to say or if he would be able to handle it. So he stuck to lighter topics.

"Good." Lisa answered, with strands of pasta and sauce hanging from her mouth.

"It tastes burnt." Becky said, nastily. "And so does the salad."

"How can salad taste burnt?" Michael responded in kind. "You don't cook salad. I may not be a great cook, but I know enough not to cook lettuce."

"It tastes burnt." Becky repeated, shoving her plate away.

Michael suppressed his anger. He tried to understand how hard it must be for Becky to lose her mother.

"Well, you've got to eat something. Have some of the bread."

"It tastes burnt." Becky folded her hands tightly across her chest.

"I didn't cook the bread! You haven't even tasted it. So how can you know if it tastes burnt?"

"It smells burnt."

Lisa giggled. Seeing her smile made Michael smile.

"I'll have some of the burnt bread." she said politely.

"Here you go." Michael said, as he passed her the bread basket. "Now Becky, what would you like to eat?"

"Nothing. I'm not hungry."

"You've got to have something. Name anything. Anything at all."

"How about pizza!" Lisa chirped excitedly.

"No." Becky remained immovable.

"Then what, Becky?" Michael patiently persisted.

At last, there seemed to be a break in Becky's dour face. "Well-l-l ..., anything?"

"That's what I said."

"How about Double Fudge Nut ice cream?" she suggested, clearly testing him.

Michael paused, considering his next move carefully. Then he stood up and announced, "Okay, road trip. Everybody up. We're going to the Dairy Barn for Double Fudge Nut ice cream."

"Ya-a-a-y!" Lisa applauded. "Can I get the pink kind instead?"

"You can have any color you like. Come on. Let's go."

❖❖❖

It was good to hear laughter. It was good to laugh himself. For the first time in a long time Michael felt he had made a right decision. Lisa was playing the clown, with pink ice cream covering most of her face and running down onto her blouse. Even Becky had to lighten up from her dark mood.

Still, Michael wondered about the long road ahead and all the mistakes to be made as a single parent. He already regretted the major mistake he made in taking off for a week following the funeral, leaving the girls with Julie, a new aunt they barely knew. He needed to be alone for a while. He needed time to adjust to all the changes. But the girls had needs too. He was unable to cope with that at the time. He was paying for it now.

He went to Cape Cod. It was Jenny's favorite place. She used to go there as a little girl with her parents. It was quite a change of pace from her life growing up in Hoboken, New Jersey. Michael, having had grown up in rural Lancaster, Pennsylvania, never quite understood what the Cape meant for Jenny.

His first time in the quiet town of Truro was on their honeymoon. He returned to relive in his mind some of those precious moments with his first and only love. They had rented a tiny cottage set in the woods. Michael couldn't get the same cottage, but he rented a similar one in the same general area.

Perhaps he was just punishing himself. He found no happiness in the memories. As he moved about the cottage, as he walked through the town, as he wandered along the beach, it all seemed empty. He felt a ghost was walking alongside him. No, less like a ghost and more like a missing piece shadowing his every move. Everything he did reminded him that he was alone.

"Hey, watch where you're flinging that cone. You got ice cream on my dress." Becky's whining brought Michael back to New Jersey.

"It was just an accident. Don't freak out." Lisa protested.

"You're an accident, you slob."

"Am not."

"Are too."

"Girls, girls. Come on, we were having a good time. Just relax and let's have fun."

"How can we have fun without Mommy? I want to go home." Becky's sour mood had clearly returned.

Michael knew that he should talk to her about her mother. He knew he should be open about it, allow the girls to work through their confused feelings. He knew what he should do. But he still couldn't do it. It was just too soon. He felt like such a coward.

"All right, I can see this was a mistake. Let's go home. It's getting close to bed time anyway."

"I'm not tired." Lisa said.

"No small wonder with all the sugar you've consumed tonight. I may have to pull you down off the ceiling to get you into your bed."

Lisa giggled. Michael smiled. At least the evening wasn't a total loss.

❖ ❖ ❖

"I want you both in your pajamas by the time I come up there. And I don't want to hear any more fighting from you two." Michael moved away from the bottom of the staircase thinking that he sounded just like his own father. He shivered at the thought.

Entering the kitchen, he gasped in despair at the mess he had created. Pots and dishes were scattered everywhere. Pieces of torn lettuce were strewn about the tile floor. While they were out, the cat had jumped up on the kitchen table and gotten into the spaghetti.

"Jedidiah, you stupid cat." he muttered. "I never did know what Jenny saw in you, you mangy beast."

The cat, cringing in the corner with a strand of spaghetti in its mouth, must have sensed Michael's intentions because it quickly ran out of the room as Michael's eyes met his.

He cleared the dishes off the table and tossed them into the sink. Then he grabbed a wet rag to wipe the table and pick up the strands of spaghetti that the cat had dumped onto the floor. As he was running the rag under the faucet, he noticed the mess he had made on the counter and began cleaning it up. He glanced up at the clock on the wall to check the time.

"How in the world did I get spaghetti sauce on the clock?" he wondered aloud. As he looked around, he saw red dots of spaghetti sauce splattered everywhere. "Oh man, it looks like a slasher movie in here."

He began to devise a way of reaching all the stains, but then was sidetracked by the mound of dirty dishes waiting to be washed. Absorbed in the soap suds, it was a long while before his brain reminded him of the reason he had glanced up at the clock in the first place.

"Oh no, I forgot to check on the kids!" He rushed up the stairs, stopped, and then began tip-toeing toward Becky's room. Carefully opening the door, he saw that she was sleeping peacefully. He watched her for a few moments, wondering what she might be dreaming of - if perhaps her dreams were of her mother. He hoped they were happy ones.

"Poor kid." he whispered softly. "You don't deserve all this."

Michael turned off her light and closed the door as he headed for Lisa's room. He was surprised to find her wide awake, sitting up in bed.

"What took you so long?" she asked sweetly.

"What are you doing still awake? It's really late."

"I was waiting for you. Tell me a story."

"Lisa, it's almost ten o'clock. You should have been asleep two hours ago."

"I don't like falling asleep alone. Tell me a story like you used to. I promise I'll close my eyes."

Michael was pleased she remembered when he used to tell her bedtime stories when he first began dating Jenny. She was only four back then. It had been a couple of years since he last told her a story, a life time ago for a little girl. But she remembered.

Now Michael had to remember. He always used to make up his stories as he went along. Now he had to remember how to do that.

"Once upon a time," he began, "there lived a beautiful little girl named Lisa."

"Oh, come on." she groaned.

"No, this isn't about you. This was a different Lisa. And you're supposed to have your eyes closed." Michael paused. "Okay. There was this girl named Lisa who used to make spaghetti come out of her nose."

"Hee-hee."

"And she could make red tomato sauce squirt out her ears."

"Eww, gross!"

"This was a talent that everyone in the town really admired because there was this dragon that used to eat people. But the dragon was afraid of spaghetti and would run away whenever Lisa would come into the room. So she became really famous as a dragon-chaser-away-er. And everyone loved her, except they didn't like to be around her because she always had spaghetti and tomato sauce gushing out of her."

"That was goofy. Tell me a real story now. A nice one."

"Oh boy. Okay, but you try and fall asleep now." Michael thought for a moment. "Once, long ago there was a land of friendly people who liked to say 'Yes'. Except for one little girl, who liked to say 'No'. Any time anyone else would say yes, she would say no. But the people forgave her and loved her anyway."

"What was her name? And don't say 'Lisa'."

"No, it wasn't Lisa."

"Was it 'Becky'?"

"No, it wasn't Becky either. It was 'Julia'. Julia was a very pretty girl, but she hid her beauty behind a frown. Everybody tried to get her to smile, but she refused."

"Why?"

"No one knew. They guessed that Julia had a secret that she was hiding behind her frown - that if she smiled the secret might leak out. They didn't know it, but they were right. Julia did have a secret. And she was afraid of smiling and letting the secret out. And that was a big shame because Julia's secret was keeping her from being happy."

"What was her secret?" Lisa asked softly.

"Shhh. Close those eyes. Her secret? Well, that's the ironic part."

"What's eye-ronic?"

"Well, it's kind of hard to explain. You see, Julia's secret was that God loved her. And she wanted to keep that love all for herself. Now, this is what made it ironic. Julia wanted to keep the happy news to herself. But by doing so, she was unhappy. If she hadn't kept it a secret, if she shared God's love with others, she would have been happy and loved. You see, it wasn't really a secret after all. Everyone else in the town knew God loved them too. That's why they always smiled and said yes."

"What happened to Julia?" Lisa asked, rolling over on her side, sleep starting to set in.

"Well, all the other people in the town kept on being nice to her. They always smiled and said yes. But Julia kept on saying no, until one day, years later, she couldn't keep the secret in any longer or she would burst. So she blurted out 'Yes'. And from that day on, Julia became one of the happiest, biggest smiling, yes saying people the town had ever known."

Michael kept quiet for a few moments, looking at Lisa lying still. Finally, he asked softly, "Are you asleep?"

"Mmmm."

"Goodnight."

"Mmmm."

Michael gently touched her hair with his hand and then got up to leave. He amazed himself by his story. With everything he was feeling, he still managed to speak of God and love to a little girl. Was he just trying to keep a myth going? Was God like Santa Claus, a story you tell to small children? Michael was too tired to dwell on it tonight. He headed for his bedroom.

It was his first night in the bed in over a month. He had been sleeping on a chair in the living room while Jenny was confined to the first floor, sleeping on the couch. He couldn't face sleeping in the bed when she died. Then, after the funeral, he took off to Cape Cod for a week. Now he was back, trying to return to normal. He hated that word 'normal'. There was no such thing. But he did need to return to some sort of routine. He undressed for bed.

Despite his tiredness, he could not fall asleep. He continued to toss and turn, looking for a comfortable position. Finally, he gave up and went down to the kitchen to finish cleaning up.

He found himself instead in the living room, in the same chair that had served as his bed for those long, painful weeks. The quiet struck him with full force. It was the moment he had dreaded. He could deal with the noise and the challenges set by Becky and Lisa. He couldn't deal with himself. Now, with the girls asleep, he had to face the silence and the reality of his own thoughts.

His mind returned to Cape Cod, the first time in Cape Cod, their honeymoon. Why was it haunting him so? He couldn't understand. But the mystery was not going to let him find any sleep tonight.

◆◆◆◆◆

As the sun lit the living room, he pulled himself out of the chair, tired, but unable to keep his eyes closed any longer. It was barely six a.m., too soon to wake the girls. Besides, it was their last day of summer vacation before school started again. Let them sleep.

Michael moved sluggishly toward the kitchen to begin contemplating a breakfast menu. His eyes focused on the walls. At first he thought his eyes were having trouble adjusting. Then he remembered that the red dots he saw everywhere were from the spaghetti sauce. He still hadn't gotten far in cleaning up the kitchen. He didn't feel like making any more of a mess. Why bother cooking? It was the last day before school. McDonald's for breakfast would be an end of summer treat.

Michael felt like making himself a cup of coffee, only he didn't drink coffee. Jenny always drank coffee in the morning - gallons of it. But there was no reason to keep the coffee maker out on the counter any longer. Everywhere he turned were the reminders. This was Jenny's house. It was hers before they met. Her presence was everywhere. Michael never had the opportunity to make any of it his. Maybe it was time to start putting some of the things away and establishing his own presence. He looked at the coffee maker. It seemed 'right' there. He went to the refrigerator and drank some orange juice from the container.

◆◆◆◆◆

A quick cold shower renewed Michael's energies enough to enable him to get through another day on next to no sleep. After getting dressed, he went down to the living room to read the morning newspaper. Once again the quietness struck him sharply. He had always been pretty much of a loner, and the quiet never used to bother him. He welcomed it. But now it brought nothing but pain. Fortunately, the flush of an upstairs toilet broke the silence and told him that he would soon be joined by at least one hungry child.

Lisa ambled down the stairs in her pink pj's, clutching her favorite stuffed animal, a soft white furred bunny that Jenny had given her the Easter before she died.

"I'm hungry. What's for breakfast?"

"Good morning. Did you sleep all right?"

"I guess. What's for breakfast?"

"I thought we'd go out to eat."

"Again? Where?"

"How about McDonald's?"

"Oboy! We're going to MacDonny's!" Lisa was jumping up and down excitedly. "When do we go? Let's go. I'm ready."

"Now hold on. First you've got to get dressed. And then we've got to wait until your sister wakes up."

Lisa tore up the stairs. Michael heard her yelling from the living room.

"Wake up, Becks. We're going to MacDonny's. Come on, get up."

"Go away. Stop jumping on my bed. Let me sleep."

"You've got to get up. We're going to MacDonny's."

"Get out of here!"

Michael thought Becky's yell could be heard throughout the neighborhood. He thought about going up to avert any further trouble, but decided to let them handle their own affairs, sister to sister.

About a half-hour later, at Lisa's constant urging, Becky came down the stairs, dressed to go, attitude intact.

"It's too early to eat. Aren't we ever going to eat at home?"

"Good morning, Becky. How did you sleep?"

"Some nerd woke me up in the middle of the night jumping on my bed." she said, shooting Lisa a dirty look.

"Did not. And it was just a little while ago anyway."

"Well, as long as everybody's up, let's say we head out for breakfast." Michael nodded his head slightly, motioning towards the front door.

"Yay!" Lisa squealed.

"Do we have to?" Becky griped.

"Yes. Let's go."

•••◈◈◈•••

Michael did not find his breakfast sandwich very appetizing. He left it half-finished. Lisa happily ate away at her meal, and Becky chewed quietly.

"Well, it's your last day before school begins. What do you want to do today?"

"Sleep." was Becky's not unexpected response.

"Let's go to the zoo." was Lisa's more helpful suggestion.

Michael smiled sadly at Lisa's choice. Jenny loved the zoo. It was amazing how much the two of them were alike. He never really cared much for zoos, but willingly went along just to be with Jenny. He didn't think he was up to it now.

"I've got a better idea." he offered. "Why don't we go to the amusement park and check out the new water rides."

"Yeah!" Lisa concurred.

"It's too cold." Becky complained.

"What are you talking about? It's not even nine o'clock and it's already 80 degrees out. Come on, it'll be fun."

Michael always loved amusement parks, from the time he was a child in Lancaster and his family would travel to Hershey Park.

But he only took Jenny to an amusement park once. She agreed to go along, but she didn't enjoy amusement parks. She preferred nature. She refused to go on any of the rides that looked even mildly dangerous, which knocked out a lot of Michael's enjoyment.

Now was Michael's opportunity to have some fun and pass on some of his childhood memories to his stepchildren. They drove down to Great Adventure, a large theme park located in central New Jersey. It was now a part of the Six Flags franchise, but all the locals remembered it by its previous name. Both Lisa and Michael were openly excited as they pulled into the entrance. Even Becky was showing signs of anticipation.

"Oh look, they have animals here." Lisa bounced in her car seat when she saw the sign with a giraffe on it for the park's animal safari.

"We're not here to see animals. We want to go on the rides." Michael hadn't driven for an hour just to see animals. He was anxious to get on some rides. The little kid in him was rising to the surface.

"I want to see the animals." Lisa protested loudly.

Michael was becoming irked. "Stop it Lisa. Maybe we can go later. First we're going on some rides."

"But I want to see garaffes."

"It's gir-affes." Becky corrected. "Knock it off."

Becky's stern rebuke seemed to do the trick in quieting Lisa. Michael was grateful. He paid the parking fee, then the admission fee.

"Okay, what should we do first? How about the water rides?"

"It's too cold."

"Let's not go through that again, Becky. Come on, I think it's that way."

They started to walk toward the right side of the park. Michael's lively pace matched his enthusiasm to get on a ride. Becky's stride betrayed her equal enthusiasm. But then Michael noticed that one set of footprints was missing.

"Oh no, where's Lisa?" Panic rose up to Michael's forehead. They quickly backtracked to find Lisa slowly walking around in confusion, fear rising to the surface of her face.

"Lisa, what happened to you?" he said, relief in his voice.

"I can't walk that fast. You left me." Tears began forming on her face.

Realization came to Michael that he was not just a kid in an amusement park. He was an adult with responsibilities. He didn't like the realization.

"I'm sorry, honey. Here, hold my hand. We're almost there."

The first ride they came to was Raging Rapids, a ride in a large raft down a rapid flowing river. Michael led them in line. After a 15 minute wait through a winding line, they got onboard a raft with seven other people. It was a circular raft which spun them around as they made their way down the river. Water continually splashed up over the boat, soaking their feet. Becky seemed to be enjoying the ride. But Michael couldn't enjoy it because he felt embarrassed by Lisa's panicked screams throughout the ride. She was still crying as the ride came to a stop.

"What are you crying about?" Michael asked as they left the ride.

"It was scary." Lisa cried.

"That? You can't be ..." Michael stopped himself. He had forgotten the age difference and now he was trying to see the ride from a six year old's perspective. "Okay, I guess that was a mistake. Let's try to find something simpler."

They came to the next nearest ride, Splash Water Falls, a combination of a roller coaster and a log flume ride.

"Oh, this looks great. We've got to do this." Michael had already forgotten to take into account Lisa's young age. He was too excited about enjoying another ride.

"I don't want to go." Lisa proclaimed. "I want to see the animals."

"How about you, Becky? Do you want to give it a try?"

"I guess."

For a split second, Michael considered getting on line with Becky, leaving Lisa behind. But immediately he realized he couldn't leave Lisa alone. He was stuck. He couldn't go on the ride without her, but he couldn't take her on the ride either. He was determined to get on the ride. The only way he could do it was to convince Lisa that it wouldn't be that bad.

"All right, let's just stand here and watch the ride for a while." He pointed to a car just starting out on the ride. "See, look. You just sit in that car and it takes you around in a circle. See how slowly it's going."

"I don't like the hills." Lisa protested.

"Watch. There's only one little hill, right there. Here comes the car. Watch it go down."

The car, carrying about 15 people, approached the hill, and then took a downward plunge, spraying water out in front of it.

"See, that wasn't so bad."

Lisa was still frightened of the fall, but the spray of water fascinated her. She agreed to give it a try.

After another long wait on line, they got on the ride and began up the hill. Lisa was doing her best to hold back the fear. It wasn't long before they reached the crest of the hill and began their rapid descent. Lisa and Becky both screamed, but their screams turned to laughter as a wave of water went forth before them."

"You see, that wasn't so bad. We didn't even get wet." Michael said, a bit disappointed.

They got off the ride and looked for the exit. There were two ways of going. Michael wasn't sure which way was the right way to go. Some people were exiting to the right, while others were going on straight ahead. Michael stopped someone passing him and asked what was ahead to the left.

"It's where the wave from the ride comes up and splashes you." the teenaged boy answered hurriedly, as he continued walking. "There's a platform to stand on that gets you soaked."

"That sounds great." Michael said to the girls. "Let's go get wet."

"I don't wanta." Lisa moaned.

"I don't either." Becky agreed.

"Okay, I'll tell you what. You stay right here where I can see you. Promise to wait right here. Don't move from this spot. I'll be right back. I just want to get wet."

The girls did as they were told, and Michael went on to see what was ahead, while constantly looking back to make sure he could still see the girls. He was half-regretting his immature decision, but he kept going. There was a group of people standing against a wall in front of the place where the car came down and hit the water. They were about 20 feet above the ride. There was a pathway in front of the wall for people to get by, with a railing for safety. Michael decided he wanted to get really wet, so he stood along the railing to be the first to feel the spray.

"You're going to get wet there, Mister." the same teenaged boy said.

"That's what I want." Michael said arrogantly, insulted by being called 'Mister'.

He watched as the car made its climb up the hill. It seemed to be taking forever, but finally it started down. Michael saw a wave of water rising up. It looked more intimidating from this angle. In under a second, the wave became a solid wall of water towering over his head, and before he could react Michael was hit full force by the water's onslaught. It knocked him back from the railing and pounded him against the wall where everyone else was standing. He would have collapsed to the ground if the water pressure hadn't held him up.

The excitement over, everyone else proceeded to the exit. Michael stood there in shock. He had wanted to get wet. Every inch of his body was now drenched. His clothes felt like they weighed about 50 pounds. The crystal of his watch was cracked. His wallet was waterlogged and all his money was like limp confetti. Another group of people assembled while he was assessing the damage. Too late, Michael realized he needed to move on. He glanced up just as another wave pounded him back against the wall.

Both Becky and Lisa broke into hysterics at the sight of Michael sloshing his way back toward them. To save face, he acted like he had intended on getting this wet all along.

"Well, what should we do now?" he asked, enthusiasm noticeably lacking.

"I'm hungry. Can we get something to eat?" Becky asked.

"Well, it's still a little early yet for lunch. And besides, I don't think they'll take my money in its present condition." He held out the sopping wet bills for the girls to see. They responded with muffled laughter.

"Can we see the animals now?" Lisa begged again.

"I'm too wet to go through the safari right now. Why don't we go and find some rides more your speed while I dry out. There's a Kiddie area around here somewhere."

They found the area that had children's rides. Michael watched as Becky took Lisa on all the rides. They both appeared to be having a great time. Michael, however, was miserable. It hadn't been anything like he expected. There were so many rides that he wanted to try out. But he realized he couldn't take the girls on any of them. And he couldn't leave them by themselves. The day was a total loss. He might as well take them through the wildlife safari.

His money had dried off enough to buy lunch. He himself was pretty much dry now, except for the squishing noises his sneakers continued to make. After eating, they returned to the car and drove through the safari section of the park. It was several miles of road, where the people stayed in their cars and the animals roamed about freely. Michael sped through it as fast as he could, passing other cars whenever possible. They drove past almost every animal known to humankind: lions, giraffes, elephants, gazelles, bears, water buffalo, and many others. Lisa kept calling for him to slow down, but Michael was bored out of his mind. He couldn't wait to get out of there.

He was forced to slow down when they came to the area containing the various members of the ape family. The chimps were climbing all over people's cars, causing a traffic slowdown. Lisa was beside herself with glee, watching their antics on the car in front of them. Becky also was laughing. Michael was thinking only about how he'd have to wash the car after this.

"Make the monkeys climb on our car, Michael." Lisa demanded.

"I don't want a smelly ape messing up my hood." Just as Michael said this, two of the chimps climbed onto the roof. Lisa was leaping about the car to see them. Becky was falling off her seat, laughing. Michael was shouting "Get off" and cursing under his breath. Then he noticed another chimp pulling the molding off the side of the car.

"Hey, stop that. Get away from there." He tried beeping the horn to get them off, but they wouldn't leave until the one chimp had managed to peel off the entire strip of molding.

Michael was livid, more so that the day was shaping up to be a disaster than the fact that his car was damaged. He lodged a complaint with a guard at the exit gate, but the guard informed him that the posted warning sign, which Michael hadn't bothered to read because he was driving too fast, clearly warned of the danger and absolved the park of any liability.

The girls were tired and ready to go home, but his stubborn streak refused to allow him to leave until something out of the day was salvaged. He was determined to stay to see the evening fireworks display. Since they couldn't find any rides that they could all enjoy together, they spent the rest of the day eating at the various snack stands stationed throughout the park and watching the different shows that the park put on.

The shows were Jenny's favorite part of the park. Of course, Michael hated them. It was amazing how different they were from each other. It was amazing how much they were in love despite their differences. The girls seemed to enjoy the shows as well, especially the high diving act and the dolphin program. By the time the fireworks display began after sunset, they were dead on their tiny feet. The loud noise of the explosions and the spectacular colors emblazoned across the sky woke them up briefly, but they slept soundly in the car for the whole journey home.

Michael had to carry Lisa into the house and place her into bed. Becky lumbered her own way up the stairs to her room. After making sure that Lisa was sleeping peacefully, Michael checked in on Becky. She seemed to be more awake now than she did at the park. She was sitting on the edge of the bed, rather than lying in it.

"What's the matter, honey?" he asked softly. "Why are you sitting up?"

"I don't feel too good. I think I ate too much junk."

"Let's see. Besides lunch and dinner, there was the popcorn, the pretzel, cotton candy, two snow cones I believe, oh, and the fried dough, and the ice cream bar, and about five sodas. No more than the usual amusement park allotment."

"You let us eat too much junk food. You need to take better care of us."

Michael was taken aback by the wisdom of this little girl reminding him that he had responsibilities to start living up to. "You're right, honey. I'll try to do better. Does your tummy hurt?"

"A little."

Michael sat on the bed beside her and checked her forehead. He wasn't sure why. It was just something he thought was expected of him. So were his next words. "Your head doesn't feel hot. Do you feel like throwing up?"

"I don't know."

"Why don't you lie back for a little while, see how your tummy feels." Michael propped up her pillows against the headboard and helped her move back. Then he placed the covers over her. "Do you want me to stay here for a while?"

"No, that's all right."

Michael studied her face. "Is there something else bothering you?"

"No." she replied, with no inflection.

"Are you worried about starting school tomorrow?"

"No."

It was not a convincing no.

"You sure?" he asked again.

"I don't know."

"What is it?" Michael sat by her feet.

"Nothing."

"It sure sounds like something. Come on, talk to me."

"I'm afraid."

"Afraid of what?"

"They'll make fun of me."

"Who?"

"The other kids."

"Now why would you say that? You've always liked school. You had a lot of friends last year. They'll all be there again this year. You never had any trouble before. Why would you have any trouble now?"

"'Cause I don't have a mother."

"Oh Becky." Michael moved forward and caressed her hair as he thought about his next words. But his tongue was moving faster than his mind. "You do have a mother. She may not be with us now. But she's still inside us. And I'm sure she's watching over us now in heaven."

"How do you know?" Her tone indicated that she really wanted an answer.

How did he know? Somehow he had to believe it even if he wasn't sure of his own faith. He needed to believe it, and he needed to convey that faith to Jenny's daughter.

"I just do." he found himself saying. "Faith tells me to believe. Don't worry about the kids in school. I'm sure they won't make fun of you."

"What if somebody asks me about my mother?"

"Tell them the truth. You tell them your mother is Jennifer Farley Griggs, and she loved you very much. But she's in heaven now, watching over you. They won't make fun of you. Trust me."

"I guess."

"How's your stomach now?"

"A little better."

"Good. Okay, why don't you close your eyes? Morning will be here before you know it. You don't want to oversleep and miss your school bus. Goodnight."

Michael got up to leave. Just as he was about to turn off the light, he heard Becky speak softly to herself.

"We shouldn't have had fun today."

"What's that?" He started back toward her bed.

"We shouldn't have had fun. It wasn't right."

"What are you talking about?" He was genuinely confused.

"At the amusement park. We shouldn't have gone."

"Why not?"

"Because I had fun. I shouldn't have had fun. It wasn't right."

Michael was confused by the agitation in her voice. "Becky, I don't understand. Why shouldn't you have had fun?"

"Because Mommy wasn't there. She's dead."

"Becky, we just talked about that."

"But if she's in heaven watching us, she saw us having fun. How do you think she feels seeing us laughing instead of being sad?"

Michael was beginning to understand. Once again, he wondered about the wisdom of imposing religious myths on young children. His own confusion was flooding back into his thought process. But right now he needed to say something to help Becky. He struggled through his words.

"I bet your mother was very happy today, laughing right along with you. I think your mother wants us to be happy. Don't you think it would make her more sad to see us being sad?"

"But it's not fair. She should have been with us. She should be here now, not ..."

"Not me?" Michael finished her thought.

"Why did God have to take her? Why'd she have to leave us alone?" Becky's tears began to flow, breaking Michael's heart all over again.

He put his arms around her, putting aside the sting of her rejection of him. It had been there just below the surface waiting to come out. It finally had. He understood her pain and her resentment of him. He felt the same resentment toward God.

"I miss her too." he said. "I want her back. But there's nothing any of us can do to make that happen. We've got to find some way to go on."

"Can I stay home from school tomorrow?" she sniffed, as her tears subsided.

Michael wasn't sure what the wise answer was, but he truthfully didn't think he could face her for another full day.

"I don't think that's a good idea, Becky. You need to get back to a normal routine. We all do. Believe me, it's better that way. It will take your mind off … some things."

He stopped to get a grip on his own emotions, then continued. "I know it's been real hard for you. I understand that you've been feeling bad about having a good time without your mother. You feel that you need to be sad all the time. But you don't. Your mother wouldn't want that. No one can take too much sadness. We all need some happiness to help us through the hard times. That doesn't mean that you don't still miss your mother or forget about her. Like I said, there'll always be a part of her inside you. But after a while, the good memories will be stronger and it won't hurt as much. I promise."

Becky seemed to be much calmer now. Maybe at last she'd be able to fall asleep, and maybe at last the barrier that she had placed between them would break, at least a little. It would sure make his life easier. To think, Becky had been the reason he and Jenny had gotten together in the first place. The memory brought an ironic smile to his face. It looked like he could leave and let Becky go to sleep.

Once again, Michael was left with the dreaded quietness. He was determined to get some sleep this night, and to do it on a bed this time. He went to the bedroom and got undressed. But the sleep wouldn't come. Instead, the memories came to visit. Again, he found himself in Cape Cod, on the beach. Jenny was with him, playing in the surf, speaking to him. But he couldn't hear what she was saying.

Why? Why couldn't he hear her, and why was he obsessed with this particular memory? Somewhere there was a key that would unlock the full memory. But he couldn't find it. It was too frustrating. He tossed about on the bed violently. He needed to focus on something else, anything else.

He made himself relax. His mind took him back, back to the beginning. Everything was vivid in his recollection. He was about to meet the girl of his dreams, the true love of his life.

CHAPTER ONE

then

He was excited about coming to Holmdel, New Jersey. As he left the turnpike and followed the directions which led him along the winding roadways of Holmdel with its many horse farms on either side, he was reminded of his own town of Lancaster, Pennsylvania. But he knew that there would be many differences as well. He had always been a small town boy, and Holmdel was no small town. It was an area in Central New Jersey containing many large, expensive houses. Most of the population was not comprised of farmers. Many of the residents had high profile jobs in New York City and commuted to their palatial homes in the suburbs. Many others worked for the large Pioneer Labs facility in Holmdel. It would be a new experience for him. He was anxious to get started.

He found Lord of Love Lutheran Church with no difficulty. The building was much bigger than he expected. He was used to the small Lutheran churches that dotted the countryside of rural Pennsylvania. This expansive complex spread out along the enormous parking lot. It was all one-story, but the sanctuary itself towered above the rest of the building, with its large octagonal shaped roof reaching toward the heavens. He took a moment to take it all in before going inside. This would be where he would be spending most of his time for the next year in his life. A year of internship under pastoral supervision to test his wings as a minister before returning to seminary for his final year of education. It was time to begin. He headed for the entrance.

He found the church office just to the right of the entrance without a problem and introduced himself to the woman behind the desk of the large office.

"Hi, I'm Mike Griggs. I'm the seminary student who's supposed to be doing his internship here."

"Come in Mike." the woman smiled. "We've been expecting you. I'm Karen Clark, the church secretary. Welcome to Lord of Love. We're looking forward to having you here."

Michael was impressed. Most of the church secretaries he had seen were gray haired little women in their seventies with floppy dresses and hearing problems. Karen looked to be in her early forties, and she was attractively attired in a business outfit. New Jersey was different.

She led him into the adjoining pastor's study where the minister was seated at his desk. Michael had met him once before at his internship interview at Gettysburg Seminary. He was a tall man, slightly overweight, in his mid-sixties. His hair was a mixture of charcoal and silver. He stood up to greet Michael.

"Hello Pastor Nordtveit. It's nice to see you again."

"Call me Eric, Mike." he said, shaking Michael's hand. "Do you prefer Mike or Michael?"

"Everyone just calls me Mike."

"Good enough. Have a seat and we'll chat awhile about the congregation."

Michael and Eric talked for a good hour and a half about the church, its people, and what would be expected of Michael over the next year. Their conversation was interrupted by a woman standing at the doorway.

Something about her intrigued Michael. She was slender, as was Michael, and a little shorter than his five foot ten inch frame. She had straight hair, curling slightly at the shoulder. It was the same light brown color as his. But her eyes were nothing like his hazel color. They were a deep brown, and she had a penetrating look. They gave life to her slightly rounded face.

Her clothes were another matter. Michael had never seen anything quite like it before. She was wearing long black zippered boots, which ended just below her kneecaps. He caught a glimpse of black stockings at the knee before fixating on the long, red plaid jumper that began just above the knee and ended high at the waist. It was topped by a thick black belt with a large gold buckle. She wore a white blouse which puffed out at the sleeves. She was wearing a black beret on top of her head, shoved toward the back.

"Excuse me." she said in a low, delicate tone. "Pastor, I just wanted to let you know that I was here working on the cookbook."

"Come in." Eric said. "I want to introduce you to someone."

The woman entered the office, and Michael stood to greet her.

"This is our new intern that I was talking about, Michael Griggs. Mike, I want you to meet one of our most active and valuable members, Jennifer Farley."

"Hello." she said, not paying him much attention, extending her hand, but not really looking at him.

"Nice to meet you, Jenny."

"It's Jennifer." She immediately brought her attention back to Pastor Nordtveit, exchanging a few more comments about the cookbook before excusing herself in order to get to work.

His first day as an intern had turned out to be pleasant, though certainly not momentous. After talking to Eric for a while, he was given a tour of the community and then had lunch with Eric and his wife, Jane. Eric then had other things to do, so Jane drove Michael to the apartment where he would be staying for the next year. Michael spent the rest of the day settling into his new place.

The entry door opened into a large living room with a kitchenette and dining area at the rear. Behind that was the bathroom and bedroom. Nothing fancy, but his first real place. It certainly beat all the years spent living in a dorm room.

After unpacking his things, Michael went out to buy some groceries. He then made himself a frozen dinner. It was the first meal he had ever cooked, if you counted heating up a frozen meal in a microwave as cooking. It was the most momentous thing of his day.

He settled in a chair to read for a while. Everything was quiet. Michael loved the quiet of the evening. He loved the solitude and the chance to relax and do some thinking. He thought about some of his friends from seminary and wondered how they were making out on their intern placements. His best friend, Lee Nager, was not going out on internship, but would be starting the September term at the seminary in one week. He couldn't wait to give him a call to see what was new on the seminary campus and to talk about their mutual love of The Beatles. It wasn't long before he felt tired enough to get a good night's sleep. He retired to the bedroom.

As soon as his head hit the pillow, his mind, as it always did, began to replay the events of the day. It had been a long day since he first drove off from his parents' house in Lancaster at sunrise to keep his appointment with the pastor in Holmdel. Eric seemed like a nice enough guy. And the secretary, Karen, was very nice to him. Then there was that strangely dressed girl, Jenny. She was kind of cute, though.

But he wasn't here to get involved with anyone. He was here to learn how to be a minister. Still, he hadn't really dated anyone since he started seminary two years earlier. It had been a long time. But it wasn't a good idea to get involved with anyone locally. He was only here for a year. Then it was back to Gettysburg for another year of school before beginning his ministry in a small church in Central

Pennsylvania. He had his future all mapped out. He didn't need any distractions. She was cute, though.

❖❖❖

Michael was up early to start his first full day as Lord of Love's intern. The evening's rest had refreshed him. He took a quick shower, grabbed a sip of orange juice from the container in the refrigerator, gulped down a doughnut, and was soon on his way to his new office - his very first office. He was feeling important. He was feeling grown up; well, actually more like a kid playing grown up. He couldn't wait until he got to the church.

Karen was already at work behind her desk when he arrived at 9:30 a.m. She told Michael that the pastor had been in looking for him to take him on a hospital call, but went on without him. Suddenly, Michael felt lazy.

On his way to his office at the other end of the hallway, he saw a group of women in one of the classrooms. He went back into the main office to ask Karen what was going on.

"Oh, that's the cookbook ladies." she explained. "The church is compiling a cookbook of members' recipes to sell in order to raise money for our World Hunger Appeal. Jennifer Farley is in charge of the whole project. I believe you met her yesterday. It was all her idea, and she put the whole thing together. She's an amazing girl. Would you like me to introduce you to the ladies?" Karen offered.

"Okay, sure."

They went into the classroom together. Michael recognized Jennifer at the center of six women busy collating different colored paper. She was much younger than the other women, who seemed to be of a post-retirement age. Michael noted that she was dressed slightly less eccentrically than the previous day. Today, she was wearing a gray corduroy pants suit with the same black boots. She had on a light pink blouse under her vest.

"Girls." Karen called into the room. Things quieted down as everyone turned toward her. "I have someone here that would like to meet you, our new intern Mike Griggs."

The women put down their work and flocked around Michael. Except for Jennifer. She continued working, after saying a polite hello.

After the initial pleasantries, and Michael's endurance of the typical "You're too young to be a minister" comments, Michael turned the conversation to the cookbook project. They explained how it was all Jennifer's doing and how the money they raised was going towards World Hunger. Then they showed him the pages of recipes all spread out on various tables. There were some 400 pages in all, and they were collating them all by hand. They had about 40 books put together so far. They had about another 460 books to go.

"That's quite a big job you have there." Michael commented. "Wouldn't it have been easier to use one of the fund raising cookbook companies?"

"What's that?" one of the women asked. "We never heard of that."

"There are companies that do this sort of thing professionally." Michael explained. "For a small fee, they put the whole book together. All you do is give them the recipes. They do all the rest."

"Why didn't anyone tell us about this before?" another woman gasped. "We've spent four months typing this thing up. We didn't know anything about a cookbook company. Did you know anything about a cookbook company, Jennifer?"

"We decided to do it ourselves." Jennifer said icily, staring at Michael with deep, penetrating eyes.

Michael immediately knew he had made a big mistake. He quickly bid the women well on their collating, and escaped from the room. He retreated to his office.

Michael's office was really one of the small classrooms converted for his use. It was simple, with a metal desk and an old wooden chair on rollers. There was an old beat up couch opposite his desk. There was also a shelf above his desk for his books. As he began placing some of his books from a box onto the shelf, he heard the muffled sound of children's voices coming from the other side of the wall. He decided to investigate.

Next to his office was the nursery, and there were two small children, both girls, playing with the toys in the room.

"Hello." Michael said, entering the room.

The children instantly turned dumb, and stared up at him.

"It's all right. You can talk. I'm one of the pastors here. My name is Mike. What's yours?"

The children remained mute.

"That's a neat doll you have there." he said to the girl with the light brown hair. "What's her name?"

"Veronica." said the other girl with red hair. "She's an American Girl doll. I got one too."

"Oh yeah? What's the name of your doll?"

"Betty. She's at home, though."

"I see. What's your name?"

"Rachel."

"Well, hi Rachel. What's your friend's name?"

"That's Lisa. She doesn't like you."

"Oh yeah? How do you know?"

"If she liked you, she'd be smiling."

"Oh. Hi Lisa. Can I see your smile?"

Lisa continued to keep silent. She took her eyes off Michael, and began playing with some of the other toys in the room.

"I guess not." Michael said. "Well, I guess I'd better be going. So long, Rachel."

"Bye."

"Goodbye Lisa."

Nothing.

⬥ ⬥ ⬥

Michael had sat in his office alone for about an hour when the intercom on his phone buzzed him.

"Pastor Nordtveit is back." Karen's voice came over the speaker. "He'd like to see you in his office."

Shortly, Michael was in a chair in Eric's office. Eric asked him if he had a good night's sleep, and if everything was satisfactory with the apartment. Then he gently explained that the day at Lord of Love usually began by 8:00 a.m., while at the same time making it clear with his tone under the words that he expected Michael to get in earlier from here on in. Michael said he understood.

"I understand that you've already made quite a stir with the cookbook committee." Eric said, moving on to other matters.

"Oh, you heard about that."

"The first thing you need to learn is that news travels very fast along the church pipeline. The second thing you need to learn is to be very careful about what you say because news travels very fast along the church pipeline. Still, no permanent damage done, I suppose. But be careful in the future. I don't want to lose a valuable volunteer like Jennifer Farley."

"I'll try to watch what I say from now on." Michael said. Then he changed the subject. "I do have a question for you, though. There are these two kids in the nursery next to my office. They're all by themselves. Where did they come from?"

"Oh, that must be Jennifer's two little girls. They're here all the time. They practically live here."

Michael was stunned to discover that Jennifer had children. She seemed no older than him.

Eric continued talking. "I feel sorry for those poor kids, sometimes. Their mother is always here doing something. So they just hang out in the nursery until she's done."

"What about their father?"

"Jennifer's divorced. Her husband took off just after little Lisa was born, about four years ago. He hasn't been around since. That's when Jennifer joined our church. We've given her a lot of support."

"So she's alone with two kids?"

"Yeah, but you wouldn't be interested in Jennifer. Too much baggage. We've got plenty of young single women in the congregation that you might like."

Michael was taken aback, not only at Eric's comments, but at his saying anything in the first place. Michael wasn't asking about her dating status. He was just making general conversation. Why would Eric say such a thing? It bothered him greatly.

The rest of Michael's week flowed along easily. Eric was easing him into the life of the congregation. The big day would be Sunday when he would be meeting most of the members of the congregation all at once.

There were three morning services. At the early service, Michael picked out the familiar face of Karen sitting near the front. The second service was just a blur of names and faces. At the late service, Michael remembered seeing Jennifer at the communion table, but he didn't remember her as one of the many people he greeted at the back of the church following the close of the service. He noted it, but didn't let it bother him.

Sunday afternoon, as Michael sat around in his apartment reading the Sunday paper, he thought about the morning and the several hundred faces he encountered. He didn't remember any names. It would probably take all year to match some names with faces.

One face kept popping up into his mind. Jennifer's. He thought about each encounter with her, the initial visit on Monday and the disastrous encounter on Tuesday. The image of her icy stare was ingrained onto his memory. He wished there was some way he could have taken that moment back. But he didn't do anything wrong really. Still, he should have thought before speaking.

He thought about the rest of the week. But there was nothing there. The only thing that stuck to his mind was Jennifer. Michael was too restless to stay in the apartment. But he had nowhere else to go. He didn't know the town well enough, and there was no one he really knew other than Eric and Jane. He was not about to bother them on a Sunday afternoon. So he went to the only other place he really knew, the church.

He wasn't sure why he was coming there. He only knew he couldn't stay in the apartment with his restless thoughts. As he unlocked the church door, he thought about his next move. The logical thing would be to go to his office. But instead, he went to the classroom occupied by all the cookbook pages.

He stood there for a while, looking at the room, trying to conjure up images of Tuesday morning. Ghosts walked among him. The stare faced him down. He looked at the pile of completed books. There were at most 50 books in the pile. It would take them forever to finish. He looked around at the piles of colored pages waiting to be collated. Without his brain knowing what he was doing, his hands started picking up pages.

"Maybe I can help along a little," he thought to himself, "do a few books more for them." It took him close to five minutes to complete one book. "This system is all wrong." he thought, as his mind began functioning again. "If I put all the pages that are over on that table onto this table with the orange pages, and move the other table closer to these two tables it would go much faster."

He did some rearranging. The next book took only three minutes to complete. He did a few more. Then he refined the process, moving a few more piles around. The system began to flow. He found he could do a complete book in just over two minutes. He finished about 30 books.

"Not bad." he thought. "And it's not too late. Only 5:00. Maybe I can do a few more before dinner." The next time Michael gazed up at the clock on the wall it was 8:30 p.m. He was hungry. But he was making some headway into the piles.

"There's a Burger Barn around the corner." he thought out loud. "I can get something quick from the drive-thru, and then do a few more. I'll stop at 9:00." He got a hamburger and fries, and a large coke. The surge of caffeine and sugar gave him renewed energy. He had passed the half-way mark. There were more books completed than books needing completion. If he did a few more, it would be a much more manageable task for the women to complete the rest on Tuesday. He kept on working.

It was 2:00 a.m. before Michael glanced up at the clock again. "Oh man." he thought. "I'm going to be miserable if I don't get some sleep." But he only had less than ten cookbooks to complete. He might as well go all the way now. Tiredness made the last books take much longer, but he finally completed the task and found satisfaction in it. He headed for home, no longer haunted by the icy stare.

Getting out of bed Monday morning was difficult, but Michael managed to get to the church by 8:00. He may be dead on his feet, he thought, but Eric couldn't get on him for coming in late. He went into the main office. Karen was just hanging up her coat.

"Hi Karen."

"Good morning, Mike. You look terrible. Didn't you sleep?"

"Not much. Is Eric in?"

"No. He called last night to say he wouldn't be in 'til late. There was a late night movie he wanted to see on television, so he was going to sleep in this morning."

"Oh."

Michael wasn't much use, sitting in his office. He closed his eyes and leaned back in the chair, falling in and out of sleep. He was snapped awake by the sounds of children on the other side of the wall. He quickly ran to the main office. Jennifer was standing there, drinking coffee and talking to Karen.

"Good morning." Jennifer said coolly, taking obvious note of his disheveled appearance.

"Hi. There's something I wanted to tell you about the cookbooks before you have the women come tomorrow."

"Oh?" she said suspiciously, as if expecting another unasked for suggestion.

"Well, it's just that they don't have to come tomorrow. The books are done."

"What?"

"Really. I had some spare time, so I did them."

"You're kidding." she said, moving toward the door.

She and Karen both went to the classroom to see for themselves. Michael followed behind.

"Well, I'll be …" Karen said. "They really are done. Finally."

Jennifer looked at Michael. Her eyes were much softer, almost beautiful. "Why did you … How did you … I mean … Why?"

"Well, I kind of felt bad about last week, so I thought I'd help out. It wasn't that hard."

"It must have taken you days." Karen said, and then her face took on a knowing look, suddenly understanding Michael's tired appearance.

"Not that long really." Michael said.

"Well that was really nice of you." Jennifer offered. "I can't believe they're finally finished." she said, gazing at the piles of finished cookbooks. "I can't believe you did this."

"Well, you did all the important work, getting it all together." Michael said. Then he haltingly added, "I was impressed that you put so much work into doing something to raise money for the hunger appeal."

Jennifer mumbled a thank you, and then turned away. As if dismissing Michael, she turned her attention to Karen. "So, I guess I can go home now. I'll have to call the others to tell them not to come tomorrow." She was soon gone.

Michael returned to his office to await his weekly meeting with Eric. Around noon, Karen buzzed him to let him know that Eric had called to say he wasn't coming in today. Michael picked himself up off the chair and headed for home to take a nap.

Two days later, Michael was sitting at his desk when a young girl with dark brown hair appeared at his doorway. Michael looked at her for a while. She stayed in place.

"Hi there." he said finally.

She did not respond. Instead, she continued to stare at a place above Michael's head. He looked up. Michael had an old stuffed bear sitting on his shelf with his books. It had been given to him by his mother long ago as a first communion present. It was light brown, with one ear loosely attached. Michael stood up and brought down the bear.

"Would you like to see my bear?" he asked.

She hesitated. Michael held the bear down to her eye level.

"This is Barnaby." he said. "Say hi, Barnaby." Then he said in a deep pitched voice, "Woof, woof, woof, woof."

The girl smiled and entered the room.

"Barnaby says hi." he said in normal voice.

"That's not a dog." she protested. "That's a bear."

"Yes, I know. But Barnaby was my first pet. And he's always thought he was a dog."

"Is that all he can say is 'woof'?" the girl asked.

"No. He can talk when he wants to."

"Make him talk to me."

"I can't. It's up to him. Maybe if you told him your name, he'd warm up to you."

"Rebeccah."

"Hi Becky." the bear voice said.

"Not Becky. Rebeccah."

"Oh, sorry." said the bear. "How old are you, Rebeccah?"

"Seven."

"Wow, that's old."

"How old are you?"

"I'm only two. That's in dog years, of course."

Rebeccah giggled. "Can I play with the bear dog?" she asked.

"Okay." Michael said in his own voice. "But be careful with him. He gets mean when he's mad."

Rebeccah took hold of the bear and disappeared behind Michael's desk. Suddenly, Barnaby popped up at the edge of the desk, speaking in a whiny girl's voice.

"Hi there. I'm Barnaby. What's your name?"

"Mike."

"What are you doing here?"

"Where?"

"Here."

"I'm talking to a bear."

"No. Why are you here in this church?"

"I'm a pastor here."

"No you're not. Pastor Nordtveit's the pastor here."

"Yes, but I'm the new pastor."

"No you're not."

"Yes I am. Why am I arguing with a bear that thinks he's a dog?"

"Because I said so."

"That's not a good reason."

"Don't make me mad."

"Okay, you win. But if I'm not a pastor, what am I?"

"You're a big goofus."

"Am not."

"Are too."

Suddenly, another voice entered the discussion. "Here you are, Rebeccah. I've been looking all over for you."

Michael looked over at the door. Jennifer was standing there.

"Does she belong to you?" he asked.

"Yes. This is my daughter, Rebeccah."

"You have three children?" he asked, confused.

"No, two. Rebeccah and Lisa."

"I met Lisa last week. But she was with another little girl, Rachel. I thought they were both yours."

"Rachel's our neighbor's little girl. I take care of her from time to time."

"Oh, I see." Michael said, finally piecing things all together. "You have a seven year old daughter? You look too young."

Jennifer blushed and tilted her head down. "Thank you." she mumbled. Then looking back up, she said "Come on, Rebeccah. I'm finished here. We have to go."

"I want to stay with Mike."

"Pastor Michael is busy. And we've got to go. Say goodbye."

"What's your favorite food?" Rebeccah quickly blurted out to Michael.

"Chicken. Why?"

"Mommy, can we have Mike over for dinner the next time we have chicken?"

"Well, I ..." Jennifer looked obviously trapped.

Michael picked it up on her face and tried to help her out, even though he felt stung by her reluctance. "That's all right, really. I understand. You don't have to invite me."

"No, it's all right." Jennifer said, hesitantly. "You're welcome to come ... sometime."

"When, Mommy? When?"

"Er, uh ... tomorrow, I guess. Unless you're busy ..."

"No, I'm not doing anything. I can come." Michael could see Jennifer's unease, but his desire to have dinner with her outweighed the resistance she was putting up."

"All right then. Can you come by around 6:30?"

"How about five, Mommy?" Rebeccah piped in.

"Uh ..."

"Six thirty will be fine." Michael said, not wanting to push it too far.

"All right. I'll ... We'll see you then. Do you need directions?"

"I can find it." Michael did not want to tell her that he had driven by her house the day before to see where she lived.

"Come on, Rebeccah. Let's go." Jennifer led the girl out of the office.

Michael had a feeling Rebeccah was about to be in trouble. But he couldn't help feeling good. His smile did not want to go away.

⬥⬥⬥

Michael's mind was not on much of anything else as he waited for the time of his dinner engagement to arrive. When he got home early that evening he tried on various outfits, but nothing felt right. So he headed out to the nearest mall to find something appropriate. He did not see Jennifer at the church at all the next day. He left work early again to shower and change before heading out to her house. He arrived about 45 minutes early, so he drove around the neighborhood until 6:30 arrived. He pressed Jennifer's doorbell just as his digital watch changed from 6:29 to 6:30. Rebeccah answered the door.

"Hi Mike." she said excitedly. "Did you bring Barnaby?"

"Nope, I'm afraid not. He doesn't like chicken."

Jennifer appeared at the door wearing a pink, fuzzy sweater and a simple black skirt.

"You're early." she said.

"Gee, by my watch I'm right on time. What time do you have?"

"Six-thirty. But nobody shows up at the exact time they're invited."

"I didn't know that. I always show up on time. I hate to be late."

"Well, come in." she grumbled.

Things weren't going well. Michael stepped into the house and saw Lisa watching a cartoon on television. It was a small house. The front door led into an open living room/dining room area. The kitchen was to the left of the dining area. Stairs to the right led up to the bedrooms. There was thick carpeting on the floor, gold and black in color. The television in the living room sat on a simple wood and metal stand. Lisa sat on a wood and caned rocking chair. There were two end tables made of a silver hued metal with smoked glass tops. A matching coffee table stood in front of a zebra striped couch. The only other piece of furniture was a beat up looking upholstered black chair. A couple of flower baskets with dying plants hung from the bay window on rope hangers. The walls were a dull white, and liberally decorated with children's handprints and crayon marks.

"Doesn't the house look clean?" Rebeccah chirped. "Mommy and me spent all day today picking up all the mess."

"Rebeccah, why don't you watch TV with your sister for a while." Jennifer said, nudging her gently away. "Don't mind her. We just picked up a couple of newspapers here and there. Can I get you something to drink?"

"Soda would be good if you have it."

"Oh, we don't keep soda in the house. It's not good for the girls to drink a lot of sugar. I thought you might like a glass of white wine."

"I don't drink."

"Oh."

Things really weren't going very well.

"Well, if you'll excuse me. I need to check on how dinner's coming." Jennifer exited into the kitchen.

Michael sat on the couch and waited. Lisa kept stealing quick glances at him, but wouldn't talk when Michael tried to engage her in conversation. Rebeccah became absorbed in the cartoon. It was a long wait.

"Okay, dinner is ready. Come to the table." Jennifer announced about 20 minutes later.

The girls sat at their places. Michael took the empty seat. He looked at some sort of crusted pie at the center of the table. Dessert already? No, it couldn't be. "I hope it isn't chicken-pot-pie." he thought to himself. "I hate that. Why can't anyone ever just make plain chicken? That's all I ask."

"Rebeccah, will you say grace?" Jennifer asked.

"No, I don't want to."

"Why not? You always say grace."

"I'll do it." Lisa said. It was the first time Michael had ever heard her voice without a wall standing between them. She bowed her head, folded her hands, and said, "Thanks God. Amen."

"Thank you, Lisa." Jennifer said. She then cut into the pie. "I hope you like spinach quiche. Chicken seemed too plain, so I wanted to make something special."

"It looks great." Michael smiled. He hated spinach. He didn't know what quiche was, but he was sure he didn't like it. Jennifer plopped a big mound of it on his plate. Michael kept smiling, and asked for a glass of water. He knew he'd need something to wash down the quiche with.

Lisa came to life at dinner, eagerly eating away at her food and talking non-stop to her sister, and interrupting her mother regularly to ask questions. But she never talked to Michael directly.

"How's your quiche?" Jennifer asked Michael.

"Very tasty. I love it." He hated it.

"Would you like some more?"

He was already gagging on what he had. "Sure, why not."

She heaped another mound onto his plate, emptying the pie tin.

"I guess I should have made two quiches." she said.

Michael was thankful she hadn't.

Jennifer had the girls clear the table after dinner.

"Would you like some coffee?" she asked Michael.

"No thanks. I don't drink coffee."

"You don't drink much, do you? What would you like?"

"Water's fine."

"Yes, you certainly do drink a lot of water. You had so much at dinner, I'm surprised you didn't float away."

Michael smiled awkwardly.

"Can we have dessert now, Mommy?" Lisa asked.

"I suppose. Get the ice cream out so it can thaw out a little."

Finally, something that Michael liked.

"I thought that I'd give them their dessert now, and then we can eat later, after they've gone to bed." Jennifer told Michael. "I've made something special for us. Cheese fondue."

Michael smiled. He vaguely knew what fondue was. He'd rather have had the ice cream.

Nothing about the evening had gone the way Michael had envisioned it in his head. He was beginning to lose all interest in Jennifer. But then he watched her as she put the girls to bed. For the first time, he saw the glimmer of warmth that he had suspected was there take full bloom. He saw her mothering side, and once again he was impressed by this woman. He was also envious of the loving relationship this family of three had together. It was something that had been missing from his own childhood. Somewhere inside of him, there was a craving for this sort of relationship in his own life.

Finally, the evening took a turn for the better. After tucking the girls in, Jennifer returned to the living room and turned down the lights. She put on some music and lit several candles.

"I've always loved candlelight." she said, almost to herself. She sat on one end of the couch. Michael was seated at the other end. "I hope you like Art Garfunkel." she said, referring to the record she was playing. "I'm not so much into the artists of today. I like the older, softer stuff."

"It's nice." For once he wasn't lying. He found himself distracted, however, by the old fashioned turntable and that she was playing an actual vinyl record.

"So how do you like our church so far?"

"It's great. I really like it. The people are very friendly."

"That's what I liked about the church when I first came here."

"How long have you been a member here?" Michael already knew the answer, but he wanted to hear how much information she was willing to share.

"I came about four years ago when I had Lisa baptized."

"Lisa's about four?"

"She just turned four in July."

"And Becky's seven?"

"Rebeccah. Yes. She just had her birthday last month."

"Where were you before you came here?"

"Hoboken. That's where I grew up. That's where I met my husband, John. We moved here to get a new start. John had a great new job offer. He decided to take off for California instead to be an actor."

"Your ex-husband's an actor?"

"Who knows? I haven't heard anything from him since he left."

"And you've been bringing up Becky and Lisa by yourself."

"They're great. We have the best times together. Still, it gets a little lonely sometimes. Especially the nights, when they're asleep."

"It must be hard for you." Michael found himself slipping into his pastoral mode of active listening.

"I haven't noticed. Just having Rebeccah and Lisa in my life has made it all worthwhile."

"That's a great attitude. What do you do to support yourself?"

"I'm a dancer."

"Oh really?"

"Well, yes and no. If you ask me what I am, I'm a dancer. I dance in all the local stage productions. It's what I always wanted to do. It's what I was doing before I got married." Jennifer's thoughts appeared to be drifting to other places. She took a sip of wine before continuing. "But how do I support myself? Dancing doesn't exactly pay the bills. So I work as a waitress in a diner. It pays enough for the babysitter and most of the bills."

Michael's attention was diverted by the music playing on the record player. "Didn't that song already play just a little while ago?" he asked.

"Oh, I moved the lever thing on the stereo so that this side of the record will keep repeating after the side is finished. I can change it to the other side if you want."

"That's all right. I don't mind hearing it again."

"This is my favorite side. He's got such a nice voice. So, let's talk about you for a while, Michael."

"Well, for one thing, I like to be called Mike."

"Really? You don't look like a Mike. Mike sounds like a little boy. Michael sounds so much more mature."

"It doesn't matter to me. I answer to most anything. How about you? Do people call you Jenny?"

A look of horror came over her face. "No one ever calls me Jenny. I've always gone by Jennifer."

"Really?" he teased. "To me, you look like a Jenny. It fits you so well."

"I would never answer to anything but Jennifer."

"Nope. You're a Jenny. Trust me. You'll see."

From that moment on, to Michael she would always be Jenny. No other name would do as well.

CHAPTER TWO

now

"Come on girls. The bus will be here soon." he called up from the bottom of the stairs. "You don't want to be late for your first day of school."

The words came out automatically. "Wow, I really have become my parents." he thought to himself, laughing slightly at the realization.

Becky and Lisa came down together, dressed for school. They had picked out their own clothes. Becky was wearing her favorite dress. Lisa had on a pink top with Hello Kitty on it and bright yellow tights. He thought about having her change, but decided it was a battle not worth fighting. They picked out their favorite cereals and ate at the kitchen table while Michael finished packing their lunches. Just as everyone finished, the school bus horn tooted.

"There's the bus. Here are your lunches. I'll see you when you get home. Have a fun first day. Don't get into any trouble."

In a flash they were out the door and Michael was alone again. No time for dwelling on the loneliness, he thought. It was time to get to work. Since turning down the call to his first congregation Michael had been contemplating where life would take him. He still had some money in the bank, money left to him from a life insurance policy set up for him by his mother. It had gotten him through college and seminary, and would likely last him another six months or so. But if he wasn't going to be a minister - money wasted on an education for nothing, his father said more than once - he would have to do something to make a living and support himself and the girls.

He had always been good with his hands. He always enjoyed working with wood, though he hadn't enjoyed his time working in his father's construction business. He wanted to make furniture. He hoped he might be able to make a living at it. He figured he had about six months to give it his best shot before having to seek other employment.

The first step was to clean out the garage. It was his plan to convert it into a workshop. But first he had to sort through all the boxes stored there by Jenny over the years. He was not looking forward to the task. It would be like an archeological expedition – exploring the past, Jenny's past. A past that he realized he really didn't know that much about.

He stood in the kitchen, hesitating to hit the garage. Maybe he should finally clean up the kitchen first. He looked at the mess. The spaghetti sauce stains were still there. No, he'd rather tackle the garage.

It was not as painful as he had thought it would be. In fact, he found comfort in exploring the part of Jenny that had existed before they met. There were papers and other mementos from high school. They revealed a young girl enjoying life. He wished he had met her then. The most difficult part of his exploration was the box containing the time spent with Jenny's first husband. There were some painful photographs of her looking happy with another man. "So that's what he looks like," he thought. "He would have to be so much better looking than me." he sighed.

Fortunately, there was not much to be found in the box. It didn't look like there was much Jenny found from that part of her life worth remembering or holding onto.

The last box Michael explored was actually a large plastic container, placed high on a shelf, setting it apart from the other cardboard boxes. It turned out to be a true treasure trove. There were all sorts of items marking the introductions of Becky and Lisa into the world. Baby books, baby booties and baby blankets, shoes, and other tiny clothing items. But the best parts were the photographs. Jenny was absolutely glowing, radiating happiness holding little babies in her arms. He couldn't figure out which photos were of Becky and which ones were Lisa. He just knew they weren't the same baby in each picture, based on the different hairstyles Jenny had in the different photographs.

He had intended on tossing most of what he found in order to make room for his workshop equipment, but found very little that he could bring himself to get rid of. He couldn't even toss the photos of the ex-husband, as Jenny was also in each picture. He did contemplate getting a pair of scissors and doing some editing of the pictures later, however.

Instead, he consolidated some boxes and rearranged them to clear up some space. There was some old furniture and old toys that hadn't been touched for ages taking up room that he was able to get rid of. As long as he kept his car in the driveway there would be enough space to set up his workshop. Now he just needed to retrieve his tools and equipment from the storage shed a member of Lord of Love had allowed him to use. Three or four trips should prove sufficient to transfer everything.

He looked at his watch. It was 2:00. He had no idea so much time had passed. He thought it was still morning. He had worked through lunchtime. Suddenly he felt very hungry. The girls' bus would be bringing them home soon. There was no time to get his stuff. It would have to wait until tomorrow.

He went into the kitchen to make a sandwich. But before he could take his first bite, the doorbell rang.

"Who could that be?" he thought. "It's too soon for the girls to be home."

He opened the front door. It was the mail carrier with a certified letter that needed his signature. It was a thick envelope.

"Now what's this all about?" he wondered as he studied the outside of the envelope. It looked like it was from some law firm.

"More paperwork to do with Jenny's death?" he guessed as he carefully opened the envelope and unfolded the thick mound of papers inside.

"What the ..."

He shifted through the pages rapidly, then went back to the beginning and tried to read through the legalese more carefully. But his mind was racing too fast to concentrate on any one full page. His hands began to shake. He felt dizzy. He felt confusion. He felt outrage.

"They're trying to take away my kids." he screamed out to the empty house.

CHAPTER THREE

then

T he night wore on in casual talk. No new discoveries made, just pleasant conversation. Finally, talk gave way to silence. Michael and Jenny sat on opposite ends of the couch, under the candlelight's spell, listening to the same side of an Art Garfunkel album playing over and over again on the turntable. Neither felt a compulsion to get up and change the record.

After a while, Michael discovered that Jenny had fallen asleep. He took the opportunity to study her face in the candle's glow. She was beautiful. Michael knew that this was the woman he wanted to spend his life with. Jenny slept on in bliss.

Michael glanced at his watch. It was after eleven. Jenny had been asleep for almost an hour, and it didn't appear that she was going to wake up anytime soon. He wasn't quite sure what to do. He knew he should be going. But he didn't want to wake her. He sat awhile longer.

Finally, the endless repetition of the same album side had gotten to be too much. He got up slowly so as not to shake the couch. He turned off the stereo, and blew out the candles after turning on the living room light. After one more lingering stare at the sleeping figure, he took his leave, carefully closing the door behind him, making sure it was locked. It had been a wonderful evening.

Michael was sitting at his desk the following afternoon when he heard her voice.

"Hello, Michael. Are you busy?"

"No, come in."

"I just wanted to apologize for falling asleep last night." Jenny said, as she moved over to the couch. "I don't know what happened. I've never done that before."

"It must have been the less than spectacular impression I made on you." Michael said, half-seriously.

"No, no. It wasn't that." she said earnestly. "I was having a nice time. I guess it was just that I was feeling comfortable around you that I felt I could drift off to sleep. Don't take that in a bad way. I haven't felt comfortable around anybody like that in a long time. I felt secure with you around. It was nice. Am I making any sense?"

"I think I know what you mean." Michael was struggling to interpret her words as a compliment.

"Well, I'm really sorry. Thanks for locking the door, and for not taking advantage."

"Advantage?"

"Never mind. I'll let you get back to work." She stood up to leave.

"Wait!" Michael almost shouted. "Let me take you out to dinner to thank you for the meal last night."

"Uh, oh, that's really not necessary." She took a step closer to the door.

Michael heard the hesitation in her voice. She was resisting him. Maybe she didn't want to see him again, and was too polite to brush him off. He couldn't give up, though. He was going all the way on this one.

"Please, I'd really like to have dinner with you. Just the two of us. I enjoy talking to you."

"Uh, all right. When?"

"How about tomorrow?"

"No, I wouldn't be able to get a babysitter on such short notice on a Friday night."

"Saturday?"

"No, I have another da ... I have some other plans already. How about Monday?"

"Sure. Oh, wait. I have a meeting Monday night. Are you free Tuesday?"

"I suppose Tuesday's all right."

"Great. Next Tuesday it is. I'll pick you up at 6:30, if that's good for you."

"Eight o'clock would be better. That way I can make sure the girls are ready for bed before I leave."

"Eight o'clock it is then."

"Fine. Goodbye Michael." she said, eager to get out the door.

"Bye Jenny."

❖❖❖

Michael did not see Jenny at church that Sunday. He wondered if she might be avoiding him. He felt a little guilty over pushing her into having dinner with him. But he felt for sure that he could win her over if given the chance.

Monday morning Michael had a visitor to his office.

"Good morning Michael."

"Hi Becky. It's nice to see you. Why are you being so formal today?"

"Huh?"

"You called me Michael instead of Mike. You sound like your mother."

"Mommy says I haveta call you Michael from now on 'cause you're almost a pastor. And you're supposed to call me Rebeccah."

"But I like Becky better."

"Well, okay. Just don't tell Mom."

"You got it. Missed you in church yesterday."

"Mommy got home real late Saturday. She had a date. She got up too late for church."

"I see." Michael felt a sharp twinge go through his stomach. More than jealousy, he felt hurt. He knew it was unreasonable, but it was there just the same.

"Does your Mom go out a lot?" He felt terrible using Becky as a spy, but he couldn't help himself.

"I guess. I dunno. She's home a lot too. But we have a lot of babysitters."

Michael could see that he wasn't going to get any real answers from a seven year old. He dropped the subject.

"Where's your Mom now?" he asked.

"She's talking to Pastor Nordtveit. She talks to him a lot."

Michael had noticed that. He felt a small measure of jealously toward Eric.

"Aren't you supposed to be in school now, Becky?" he asked, suddenly realizing that it was a school day.

"I have a doctor's appointment. That's where we're going as soon as my Mommy's done."

"Ugh, the doctor. Are you sick?"

"Nah. I need to have a physical to take swimming lessons at the YWCA."

"Oh yeah? You're going to learn how to swim? Neat." Michael had never learned to swim himself. He didn't go near the water much growing up.

Becky spent a little more time in his office, as Michael returned to some work he needed to finish. She eventually walked out in silence, going next door to play with her little sister in the nursery.

As Michael finished up an Adult Bible Study he was preparing, he noticed that all was quiet in the building. He checked the nursery. It was empty. He went to the main office. Karen was typing on the computer.

"Is anyone in the office with Pastor?" he asked.

"No. In fact, he's not in either. He had a luncheon appointment."

"Oh." He left the office and returned to his own desk. But he couldn't concentrate on paper work. He wondered why Jenny hadn't bothered to at least pop in to say hi. It was all very strange. He grabbed his coat and headed out.

Stopping by the main office, he called in, "I'm going to make some hospital visits. I'll be back around two." Then he headed out in his car. He played the car radio full blast to take his mind off his darkened thoughts. A Beatles' song helped brighten his mood by the time he arrived at the hospital.

On Tuesday, Michael kept himself occupied doing the work of the parish. He kept Jenny and their evening date at the back of his mind. Until 6:00. Then he headed for home and quickly showered and changed for the evening. He didn't pay as much attention to his attire this time around. He put on his favorite sweater. It was old and didn't necessarily flatter him, but he felt comfortable in it. He had decided to not overdue things. Maybe he was just going too fast for Jenny. The way to attract her was slow and easy. Let her get to know the real him. If anything real was to develop, this was the right way to let it start.

He only arrived 12 minutes early at her house this time. But he remembered what Jenny had said about not showing up right at the hour, so he waited until ten after eight to go to the door.

Jenny opened the door and said, "Where have you been? I'm paying this babysitter by the hour."

He was all confused. "I'm sorry. Are you ready to go?"

She quickly said goodnight to the girls, giving each of them a kiss, and they were on their way to the restaurant.

Michael chose an informal place, The Beef 'n More Beef Restaurant. He liked that they not only had all sorts of meats on the menu, but they also served, instead of rolls, a bowl of popcorn at the table which they kept replenishing. Michael was always impressed by simple little things like that. The place was family-oriented, with red and white checkerboard table cloths and cartoons displayed on large video screens.

"I've never been here before." Jenny said. "It's … interesting."

Michael quickly surmised that she was used to more fancy places with her other dates. Well, this was what he liked. He was going to show her who he was, and this was it. He wasn't going to worry about it.

It turned out to be a pleasant, relaxed evening. They got by on small talk during dinner, and gradually moved into a deeper conversation over dessert. Jenny made a passing reference to a time when she was still married, and Michael took advantage of the opportunity to find out more.

"You must have been really young when you first got married." He was dying to know just how old she was.

"Yeah, I was." She did not offer more.

Michael tried a more direct approach. "You know, I was wondering … If you don't mind my asking, how old are you now?"

Jenny hesitated for just a moment. "I'm 25. How about you?"

Michael was glad to know that she was just as curious about his age. "I'm 23." He continued, "Now if Becky's seven, then you must have had her when …"

Jenny completed his thought. "I had just turned 18. John, my ex-husband, was older than me. He was 26. He had just gotten out of the service. I was … different then. I was your proverbial wild child. I got pregnant right out of high school. We got married a few months before Rebeccah was born."

"Wow." He knew it was a dumb thing to say, but it was the only thought that would come out of his mouth.

"Wow is right. It wasn't a great marriage from the start. But having Rebeccah made me change my life for the better. I was never into the church before. My mother used to make me go to Sunday School, and I hated it. But then in the hospital after giving birth, I picked up a Bible and started reading it. I named Rebeccah after a character in the Bible. But I added an 'h' to the end of the name. I still had a bit of the old rebellious streak in me."

She casually dipped her spoon into her dessert bowl and scooped up a large portion of Double Fudge Nut ice cream. After licking the spoon clean, she continued, "John was what you'd call a lapsed Catholic. He had no use for the church, and he wouldn't let me go either. Rebeccah was almost two before I finally had her baptized in secret. John never knew. There was a lot wrong with my marriage, a lot that I'd rather just leave in the past. But I kept on reading the Bible, and it helped me get through an awful lot. Some of it really awful."

Michael could see the pain in her face, and didn't wish to push her down a painful path. He knew it wasn't appropriate to change the subject all together, so he tried to find a less painful area.

"When did you get a divorce?" He wasn't sure if this were any better an area to explore.

"Just after Lisa was born. He was real upset about me being pregnant again. It was a fluke. We were hardly ever together anymore. He didn't want me to have Lisa. But there was no way I was going along with that. It was the first time I ever stood up to him. He left the house a week after she came home from the hospital. He never came back."

"He never visited the kids?"

"No. It was difficult enough tracking him down to sign the divorce papers. After that we never had contact."

"And he never helped with support?"

"No." She laughed sarcastically.

"I'm sorry." Michael couldn't think of anything but dumb statements to make.

"It's not your problem. I'm real happy with my life the way it is now. Money is tight, but I like being in control of my own life, and I love being with Rebeccah and Lisa. I'm not looking to change anything."

Michael wondered what her last statement meant in terms of a possible future relationship. The waitress came over to the table with the check, and their conversation did not develop much beyond that point. Jenny seemed anxious to get home.

"The babysitter can't stay past eleven." she said.

They arrived back at Jenny's house well before eleven.

"Could you drive the babysitter home?" Jenny asked, after paying the young girl. "It's not far. Connie can give you directions, right?" she said, looking at the babysitter.

The girl nodded.

It felt strange for Michael to be in the position of taking a babysitter home. It wasn't that long ago that he was babysitting for his older sister's children. He was also a little upset that Jenny was putting an end to their evening so abruptly. But then, her next words made him feel positively ecstatic.

"I'll put some coffee on, if you'd like to come back."

"Sure." he said.

"Oh, but you don't drink coffee. I forgot."

"Water would be good. I'm still thirsty." Michael did not want to let the invitation slip away on a technicality.

"How about some hot chocolate?" she suggested.

"Perfect." he smiled. "I'll be right back."

He wasted no time getting back to the house after dropping the babysitter off. Jenny had the house lit in candlelight once again. Fortunately, a different album was playing on the stereo. Art Garfunkel was still floating around in Michael's head unmercifully.

He took a mug of hot chocolate from the tray Jenny had prepared and they sat on the couch.

"This is good." Michael said, after taking a sip. He picked up one of the crackers on the tray sitting on the coffee table.

"I've told you a lot about me tonight." Jenny said, breaking the brief silence. "Tell me something about you."

"Okay. Like what?"

"Well, did you always want to be a minister?"

"No, not really. It sort of came out of the blue, in a way."

"Oh?" Jenny placed her feet up, curling herself up on the couch. She appeared to be interested.

Michael continued. "I tried a lot of different things along the way. I grew up working for my dad in the construction business. He did carpentry work. But I didn't like working for my father. We never got along that well, especially after my mother died."

"How old were you when she died?"

"Thirteen."

"I was 14 when my father died."

"Oh yeah?"

They both drank their hot chocolate for a moment, seeming to get lost in their mugs.

Then Michael picked up his story. "I worked for a plumber for some time while in high school, in between carpentry jobs. Then in college, I did a number of odd job type things. I kept switching majors until finally settling on philosophy. It was the only thing that really caught my interest."

He finished his drink and put the mug down. "My father thought it was a stupid major. 'What kind of job can you get with a philosophy major', he asked. I guess he was right. There was no work after college, so I ended up back working for my father. I hung in there for the summer, hating every minute of it. I liked working with my hands, making things with wood. But we mostly only did the big stuff like building houses. It wasn't my thing. So I quit."

"And then you went to seminary?"

"Yep. All the time I was pounding nails something kept tugging at me. I was still reading a lot of philosophy. And that gradually led me toward religious subjects. I read a lot of books on different religions. We grew up Methodist, but my father stopped going after my mother died."

"I didn't know that. You didn't grow up Lutheran? So how did you end up in a Lutheran seminary?"

Michael picked up his empty hot chocolate mug. "Like I said, I read a lot of books on different religions. I really liked the things Martin Luther said. It made the most sense to me. I kind of felt lost after college, like I was drifting away from any meaning in my life. I found a Lutheran church nearby and started going to it. I was really impressed with the minister. She and I had several discussions on philosophy and religion. She knew her stuff philosophically, and she blew me away theologically. It wasn't long after that that she had me thinking about the ministry. She was the one who influenced me to go to Gettysburg Seminary."

"So now I've finished the first two years." he continued. "It's a great seminary. The courses are very interesting and challenging. And the people there are great. I've made a lot of good friends. I miss not seeing them every day. But it's also nice being out in the world and doing this with ..."

Michael looked over at Jenny. She was sound asleep.

He waited in his office the next morning for her arrival. He knew she would come. And he was right.

"Good morning, Michael."

"Hi Jenny."

"I am so sorry. I didn't mean to fall asleep on you while you were talking. I don't know what's wrong with me. I'm not like that."

"I take it you don't fall asleep on your other dates."

"No. But now you're making me sound awful. Besides, we weren't really on a date last night, were we?"

"I thought we were."

"I'm sorry. Let me make it up to you. Can you come over for dinner tonight?"

"Yeah, I'm free. I can come over. When?"

"Anytime you'd like."

"Is five too early?"

"No, that's fine. I promise I won't fall asleep this time."

Michael felt good the rest of the day. He seemed to be getting through to her. She was certainly loosening up. He made a few pastoral visits, and then returned to the church for an after school confirmation class. He went right to Jenny's house from the church.

He spent some time with Becky and Lisa while Jenny worked in the kitchen getting dinner ready. Lisa was beginning to actually speak to him, but neither girl paid him as much attention as they did the cartoons on the television screen. Finally, Jenny announced that dinner was ready.

Michael nervously approached the table. This time there were two crust-like pie things on the table.

"You liked my quiche so much last time" Jenny announced proudly "that I made two quiches this time."

"Great." Michael said flatly. "Can I have some water?"

Dinner conversation proved impossible with both girls actively vying for their mother's attention. Michael bided his time until Jenny put them both to bed for the night. Now it was their time together.

"Aren't you going to light some candles?" Michael asked, disappointed that the normal routine wasn't being enacted.

"No, I think the candlelight makes me too sleepy." she answered. "Would you like to watch some television?"

"Sure. Why not?" This was turning out to be a different evening. Had the magic already gone out of the relationship?

They watched a mystery movie, not Michael's favorite fare. The plot was too complicated to follow without paying close attention. Michael was more interested in talking.

"How long have you been working as a waitress?" he asked.

"Forever. Way too long."

"When do you find the time to work, with the kids and all?"

"Whenever I can. I usually work days while Rebeccah's in school. I drop Lisa off at daycare. But they don't need me every day. So to pick up extra money, I fill in whenever they need me. Sometimes weekends, sometimes Sunday mornings, sometimes nights. Unfortunately, paying for babysitters usually eats up most of my tips. I'd rather spend the money on the girls."

"Well, I admire you for what you're able to do." Michael said honestly. "They really love you. That's more important than things."

"Yeah. But things are nice too."

"What about the dancing you mentioned the other night?"

"Oh that." she said wistfully. "I always thought I'd be dancing on Broadway, not waiting tables in a diner."

"People do what they have to do." He immediately realized how lame that sounded. He quickly thought up another question. "What kind of dancing do you do?"

"All kinds. I started ballet when I was barely old enough to walk. My mother was a dancer. Her career was ruined when she married my father. At least that's what she always used to say. Poor Daddy. My mother really wanted me to be a ballerina. But then I saw 'West Side Story', and that was it for me. I started taking contemporary dance and soaked in everything I could. I still take lessons whenever I can."

Jenny paused for a moment and repositioned herself on the couch, looking away from the television and facing more toward Michael. Then she continued, "I was auditioning for a show off-Broadway around the time I graduated from high school. That's where I met John. He was auditioning for one of the non-dancing parts. Neither of us got called back. But we fell in love, for a little while anyway. I think that I was also trying to get back at my mother a little. I always blamed her after my father died for all the awful things she said to him when he was alive. I think they only stayed married because of me." A wistful look came over her face. "But she changed when I got pregnant. I thought she'd condemn me for repeating her own wasted past. But she showed me a lot of support. We got along great, especially near the end, before she … before she passed away."

"You lost both your father and your mother?" he asked.

Jenny just nodded.

"I remember you said you were 14 when your father died. What about your mother?"

"She died later, from cancer, about a month before Lisa was born."

"Wow." Michael said slowly. "And your husband left just after she was born."

"Yeah, fun times, right?"

Michael did not respond. But he took in every word she said, almost memorizing it. He had never known anyone who had such a sense of self that Jenny possessed. She was not a victim of fate. She was a rider of life, always embracing each moment with a positive outlook.

They sat in silence for a while, trying to make sense of the movie. But it was too late for that. They had already missed too much of the plot.

Michael finally spoke at the movie's end. "Well, that ending made absolutely no sense. Did you know that Chester was really a woman?"

Jenny did not answer. Once again she was asleep on the couch. Michael sat through the evening news and then made his usual quiet exit, following the normal routine of locking the door behind him.

Thursday morning he waited for Jenny's arrival at his office door. She didn't show. It lingered on his mind as he went about doing other things. Late that afternoon, he found himself driving towards Jenny's neighborhood. He went to the house. Jenny answered, wearing an old bathrobe. She did not invite him in.

"What are you doing here?" she asked.

"I-I just wanted to make sure you were all right after last night."

"Oh. Sorry. I just can't help falling asleep. I don't know what it is."

"It's all right, really. I don't mind. Are you doing anything tonight?"

"I'm getting ready for work. They called me in."

"Oh. Well I was wondering if you were free tomorrow night. We could see a movie or something."

"No, I can't tomorrow."

"Oh, you have another date."

"Yes." She hesitated. "Well, no. It's ... Come on inside a second." She stepped aside to let him in. The house was a mess, with toys and newspapers scattered everywhere. "You see, I have a standing date for Friday nights."

"I understand." he said sadly.

"No, you don't. Friday nights I reserve just for the girls. It's our family night. Every Friday we go to the Italian Palace for pizza."

Michael's spirits picked up. "Oh, I see. It sounds like fun. Could I join you sometime?"

"No. That is, it's just that it's family night. Family only. I get so little time with the girls as it is. It's our time to be together, just the three of us."

"I understand. I think that's good. Thanks for telling me."

"Look, I am sorry about last night, and all the other nights. I'll make it up to you. But right now I've got to get ready or I'll be late. Okay?"

"Okay." he said, heading out the door. "I'll call you."

"Better to let me call you. Goodbye Michael." She quickly closed the door behind him.

She was making him so confused that he was getting headaches thinking about it. He tried his best to put it out of his head. He concentrated on his church responsibilities. He called old friends from seminary to chat about other things. But he found himself talking to his closest friends about Jenny. The only advice they had for him was to let go before he got hurt. But he couldn't let go, at least not in his mind. He did not initiate contact with Jenny, and several weeks passed without seeing her at all. But he saw her in his mind. She would never leave.

It was late October. Michael had had several restless nights thinking of her. Jenny kept her promise and called. She called several times in fact. They had long, pleasant conversations, talking about everything but each other. She made no offers to get together, and she had an excuse for all Michael's offers. It looked like she was determined to keep Michael as a friend only. He sat at his desk working on his first sermon. A familiar voice was at the doorway.

"Hi Michael."

"Becky! What a surprise. I haven't seen you for a while. What's up?"

"Nothing." She entered the room. "How's Barnaby?"

"Barnaby's doing fine. How's your sister?"

"Good. She's in the other room."

"And how's your mother?"

"Okay." She offered nothing more.

Michael did not pursue it. He moved onto other subjects. "Are you all set for Halloween?"

"Oh yeah." she answered excitedly. "I'm gonna be a clown."

"Neat. What about Lisa?"

"She's gonna be a bumble bee. She's always a bumble bee."

"So you really like Halloween then."

"Yeah. Mommy likes it too. It's her birthday."

"Halloween? Your mother was born on Halloween?"

"Yeah."

"Are you doing anything special for her?"

"We always have a party before Trick or Treatin'. We have cake and ice cream."

"Yeah? And who makes the cake?"

"Mommy does."

"But that's not fair. It's her birthday. She shouldn't have to make the cake."

"I don't know how to make a cake."

Michael had a flash of inspiration. "I know. We can make a cake for her together."

"How?"

"Well, I'll get the ingredients, and we can make it in the church kitchen."

"Goody."

"But we'll have to figure out a way for you to get here. Let's see. Halloween is on a Saturday. Perfect. You come to our Sunday School Halloween Party, and we'll sneak off to make the cake when your Mom's not looking."

"Yay! Good idea!"

"Okay. It's a date. I'll see you next Saturday. Don't tell anyone."

"Yeah, especially not Lisa. Bye."

"Bye." His mood was brighter than it had been for weeks.

Michael didn't know anything about baking a cake, and besides, there wouldn't be enough time to make one with the Halloween Party going on. So he bought a plain white cake at a bakery, and got a can of frosting and a decorating kit. When Becky arrived, she was anxious to get started.

"Now? Now?" she kept asking.

"Not yet. Your mother's looking. Enjoy the party. I'll tell you when."

Jenny looked at the two of them huddling together in the corner, and appeared to be suspicious. Michael let Becky enjoy the games and the costume parade. Then, while the other kids were eating orange cupcakes, he and Becky snuck off to his office.

"I thought we had to cook the cake in the kitchen." she said, curious.

"There are too many people in the kitchen. We can do it all here in private without anyone seeing us, like your mother."

"Yeah, and Lisa."

"Yeah. Okay, let's get started." He opened the can of frosting and handed Becky the spatula he had taken from the kitchen. "Here, start spreading the frosting on."

Becky had a great time spreading the vanilla frosting over the cake. Of course, the cake looked terrible by the time she was finished. Michael tried to fix it up a bit by layering on more frosting to cover the worst areas.

"There, that's not so bad." he announced. "Now, what should we write on the cake?"

"How about, 'Happy Birthday, Mommy'?"

"Perfect. Okay, I'll write. You put on the sugar stars around the edges."

When it was all finished, it was not that bad. They secreted the cake out of the office and placed it on the front seat of Jenny's car. Luckily, Becky had remembered to leave one of the doors unlocked, as planned. Then Michael went to his car and produced a number of helium balloons from his trunk.

"Wow! Balloons." Becky clapped as Michael placed the balloons in the back of Jenny's car.

"One more thing." he said, retrieving a single daffodil from his car. He then placed it on the driver's seat of Jenny's car.

"Daffodils were my mother's favorite." he said to Becky. "I hope your mother likes daffodils."

"Yellow's her favorite color. She'll like it." Becky said, approvingly.

"We'd better get back inside before your mother wonders where you are."

Sure enough, Jenny was looking for Becky as they entered the building. Michael returned to his office, as Jenny got Becky and Lisa ready to leave.

A few minutes later, Jenny appeared at his door holding the yellow flower.

"Daffodils are my favorite." she said. "How did you know?"

"I didn't really. I just like daffodils better than roses. I'm glad you like it."

"And the cake. Becky told me all about what you did. It was really very nice of you. I don't know why you did it."

"It's your birthday. Birthdays should be special."

"Look, would you like to … Well, would you like to come over now for some cake?"

"I'd love it. I'll follow you in my car."

It felt great being a part of a family, taking part in a family celebration. He had never had a birthday party, not since he was a small kid. The girls were laughing. Lisa actually hugged him a couple of times. Jenny seemed to be enjoying the attention. Everything seemed right. Then it all came crashing down.

"Thank you again for the cake." Jenny said. Then she turned her attention to the girls. "You two go get washed up now. You've got cake all over your faces."

The girls left the room. Jenny stumbled around with her words before finally saying, "I really do appreciate what you did. But I'm afraid I'm going to have to ask you to leave now. I've got to get ready."

"You have to work tonight on your birthday?" he asked.

"No, um … I have someone coming over. I have a date tonight."

"Oh." His face collapsed. He felt terrible. "Okay, I understand. I'll get out of your way."

"I'm sorry." she said, as he made his way out the door.

"No, it's okay. It's your life. I don't have anything to say about it."

She followed him out the door. "Michael, wait." She paused, and he waited to hear what she had to say. "I didn't want to be alone on my birthday. It's a lonely time for me. This guy doesn't mean anything to me. We just go out occasionally. It's no big deal."

Michael didn't want to hear any of it. None of it made him feel any better. "Really, you don't owe me an explanation. I shouldn't have intruded on your birthday. It's my fault." He tried to leave.

Jenny stopped him. "But what you did was nice. It made me feel good inside. It made me feel special. But Michael, I'm not a special person."

"What do you mean by that?" Michael said with some disgust.

"I'm not someone you should be wasting your time on. You should be with someone single without any attachments."

"Why does everyone keep saying that?" he said, visibly angry. "I think I can make up my own mind about what I want. And you are special. So don't give me any of that self- put-down garbage. I want to be with you."

Jenny took in a breath. "Michael, sit down for a moment." They sat on the front step as Jenny slowed things down. "Michael, I don't care about the guy I'm seeing tonight. But I do care about you. And I shouldn't. It isn't good for me."

"Why not?"

"Because I can't take getting hurt again. And Michael, I don't want to hurt you. It wouldn't be fair."

"I haven't encountered much in life that is fair, Jenny. I've been hurt plenty of times. But it's a risk I'm willing to take. Without risk, there's no life."

"I know what you're saying. But I saw the hurt in your face when I asked you to leave. It tore me apart. And I also know what's best for me now." She took in another breath. "I just don't think we should get involved. If we can't stay friends, then maybe we should stay out of each other's lives."

"That's not what I want."

"But it's for the best. Believe me."

Michael got up and headed for his car.

"We can still talk to each other on the phone." she called from the porch. "I enjoy our talks."

"Yeah, sure." he said, starting the ignition. Didn't she realize that it would hurt him more talking to her from a distance?

CHAPTER FOUR

now

"They're trying to take away my kids!" he found himself repeating over and over as he let out all his anger, while his sister listened patiently, sitting on a stool at her kitchen island.

He had been holding in all the frustration and rage for what had seemed an eternity. He didn't want to alarm the girls. They bounded in the door within minutes of his receiving the special delivery. He immediately set the papers aside and did his best to pretend everything was normal. It wasn't easy. It was hard. Very hard. Almost too hard for him to handle. He found himself on the brink of losing it several times at the dinner table. But he kept it all in. He had to stay in the moment for their sakes.

It was another terrible night of almost no sleep. He managed to stay in bed, but he tossed and turned throughout the night. He kept it together while the girls had their breakfast, and managed a smile as he saw them off on their bus. But as soon as they were safely off, he was off as well, making the hour and a half trip to Philadelphia to talk to Julie, the only person he felt comfortable unloading his burden upon.

"They're trying to take away my kids! They can't do that. Can they?"

At last a question. It appeared Michael had vented enough and was now ready to accept another voice. So Julie stood up from her stool, grabbed her cup of coffee, and approached Michael.

"Let me try to understand the gist of this." she began slowly, calmly. "The girls' grandparents, Jenny's ex's parents, are seeking custody of Lisa and Becky."

"Out of nowhere!" Michael began his pacing around the kitchen again. "Out of the blue. I never even heard of these people. Jenny never mentioned them. I mean, it's not even her ex-husband - not John. Maybe that I could understand, a little. But this Mildred and Gerald Farley? Who are they? What right do they have to take the girls from me? As far as I know, they never even met them. Not once. Ever."

Julie picked up the glass of orange juice she had poured for Michael that he never touched and handed it to him in an effort to settle him down again. He took the glass, but continued pacing. Julie returned to her stool.

"Do you know anything about their circumstances? Maybe John never told his parents about the girls until recently?"

"I have no idea. Jenny never talked much about her ex. And like I said, she never mentioned his parents. Julie, what do I do?"

She ached to see the pain on his face and in his voice. She always felt protective of her kid brother. But her thoughts were taking her in different directions.

"Mikey, come over here. Sit down."

Michael reluctantly, but obediently, took the stool next to his sister.

"Now I don't want you to get mad at me." she started out slowly. "Understand, I'm only playing Devil's Advocate here for a moment. But I want to help you work through all this. So I'm just going to ask, are you absolutely sure this is such a bad thing?"

"What!? What are you talking about? What do you mean?"

"I'm just trying to determine if, and again, I'm just playing Devil's Advocate here, if this might not be a blessing in disguise. Are you sure you're really up to the challenge of raising two little girls all by yourself?"

"Why are you asking me this? You're supposed to be on my side."

"Oh, Mike, I am on your side. I just want you to consider what you're getting yourself into. Raising kids is hard work. I know. I've got a husband to help me with my two kids, and still it's no picnic. Do you really think you can do this alone? Do you really want to?"

"Yes." he answered without hesitation.

"All right. I can see you're getting agitated. I don't mean to upset you. I just want you to consider the future you're committing yourself to."

"Julie, I have thought about this. I've thought of practically nothing else since Jenny died. And even before I proposed to her, I weighed the whole thing out."

"All right. That's good. So you've thought about when the girls start to become young women?"

"Huh?"

"You do know that girls' bodies change. There will be certain conversations coming your way that you'll have to be prepared to deal with. I'm talking about that time of the month and bras and ..."

Michael shot off his stool.

"Julie, I am not having this conversation with my sister."

"If you can't have it with me, how are you going to have it with them when the time comes?"

"I ..." Michael hesitated. "I will. I'll do whatever I have to. I want to be ... I am their father. I'll deal with whatever comes along."

"Good." Julie got up and stood beside him, putting her hand on his shoulder. "And you know I'll be there with you. Whatever help you need. You can count on my support. After all, they're my little nieces now. I love them too."

"Thanks, sis. Look, I know it wasn't easy for you to challenge me like this. I appreciate you being here for me. But the only help I need right now is legal help to fight this court order, or whatever it is."

"Let me call Roger at work. He's got a friend who's some kind of lawyer. I'll have him set up a meeting for you."

"Thanks, Julie. And thank Roger for me too."

"It's about time my husband was good for something, kiddo. Hey, we're all family. And family sticks together, right?"

"Well, at least you've always been there for me."

"And I always will be, Mike. I always will be."

CHAPTER FIVE

then

H e tried to bury his pain in his work. Indeed, there was much to be done in the life of the parish. There really wasn't a lot of free time for dating. It was for the best, he tried to convince himself. But he couldn't get himself to believe any of it.

One of the things that took up his otherwise free time was the number of dinner invitations he received from members of the congregation. In a way, he resented the intrusion on his time, keeping him from pursuing his own interests. But it was not hard labor. It was a good way to get to know some of the people of the congregation. It also saved him having to learn how to cook for himself.

The Nelson's were an active family in the congregation. Mr. Nelson served on the Church Council, and his wife was President of the Altar Guild. Their son, David, was in the senior high youth group. Their daughter, Angela, who at 21 had just recently returned to the area after graduating college, was a volunteer Sunday School teacher. Angela had just taken a job working in the local library. She was a tall, thin girl, with long, straight black hair. She was not drop dead beautiful, but hardly unattractive either. Michael observed this while sitting across from her at the dinner table.

It was a pleasurable evening, though somewhat empty for Michael. He was an outsider to this family meal, the intern pastor making a home visit. Conversation kept on a steady, surface level. He answered the same questions about his calling that had been asked at every dinner table so far. He asked stock questions about the family's lives, making sure not to probe into anything deep.

He made his usual excuses after the dessert was served to get out of the house and end the evening, so that he could have some time for himself. However, this time he did not escape without attracting the attention of Angela. She asked several questions about his interests, and before he left she invited him to join her and some friends the following evening for a night out playing miniature golf.

Michael was reluctant to accept, but he did enjoy miniature golf. His mind quickly weighed options of plausible excuses against the reasoning that it might be fun to spend some time with people close to his own age. He agreed to go.

At home that evening, Michael reviewed the day as he lay in bed. He thought about Angela. He explored in his mind the future possibilities. But he quickly dismissed them. Had it been another time, perhaps. But the truth was that the only future he could foresee had Jenny in it. He had no idea how that future might come about since Jenny had absented herself from the picture. But some extra sense told him to have faith and not lose hope. For now, the only thing he was seeking from Angela was to gain some new friendships among his peers.

❖❖❖

It felt somewhat strange to be playing miniature golf in December. Outside, a light snow was falling. But they were perfectly warm under artificial light and forced air heat. Michael had been unaware that there were indoor miniature golf places. He had only ever played it outdoors in summer months. Once again, New Jersey was proving to be much more advanced than Pennsylvania.

Michael's observation matched his whimsical mood. He was having a great time. Playing miniature golf was always one of his favorite things to do on a date. He felt like he was back in college, like he had gone back in time five years. Angela's friends were like his old college pals. All together, they were three couples. Michael felt just a little unease about the pairings. He had imagined being more part of a group. But it was obvious that he was considered by all to be Angela's date for the evening. There was nothing he could do about it, so he tried not to let it bother him.

Michael was glad for the opportunity to have some fun without doing any heavy thinking. He took an active part in the jokes and pranks during the game. He tried to fit in with the conversation at the snack bar afterwards. Things were running smoothly enough. But Michael couldn't help keeping a watchful eye on the family at another table. For all the fun he was having, he was feeling envious of the family unit enjoying an evening out together. It only made him think more of Jenny and the girls.

He thought more about it in bed that night. It had felt like he was back in his college dating days again. But was that where he wanted to be at this time in his life? He remembered less about the bantering with Angela's friends, and more about the family he observed. Their way had more to offer for Michael. He was ready to move ahead, not go back.

•◦• ◈ ◈ •◦•

The night before was still weighing on his mind as Michael sat in his office the next morning trying to get through a bunch of paperwork. He heard someone approaching his room. An image of Jenny quickly flashed into his mind, causing his heart to race slightly.

He immediately rationalized that it wouldn't be her, but he hoped that it might be Becky.

He was surprised to see Angela bounding through the door.

"Hi Mike." she said energetically.

It sounded strange to hear his more familiar name. He had grown used to Jenny's calling him Michael.

"Angela." he said, startled. "What are you doing here?"

"I'm on my way to work at the library." she responded, tossing back her hair and smiling. "I thought I'd stop in and see if you have any plans for lunch today."

Michael found himself answering without thinking. "Nothing that I know of." he said, slightly dazed.

"Good. How would you like me to treat you to lunch then?" She did not pause to allow for a response. "Do you know where the Beef 'n More Beef is on Rte. 35?"

Michael smiled slightly. "Yeah, I'm familiar with it."

"Great!" she responded enthusiastically. "I'll meet you there at noon."

He didn't know what to say. He answered automatically. "Okay. I guess I can meet you."

Just then, he heard voices. He turned to the door and saw Jenny and Lisa at the doorway. It looked like Jenny was about to stop, but after taking a glance into the room, she kept going down the hall.

Angela had also taken notice of Jenny, as well as Michael's anxious expression. "Great." she said, raising her voice. "I'll meet you for lunch at noon." She walked toward the door, then turned in the doorway. "Oh, I want to thank you for the wonderful time we had last night. I haven't had so much fun on a date in a long time."

As soon as she walked out, Michael ran to the door. He saw Angela walking down one end of the hallway. Then he saw Jenny walking down the other end. Had she heard? How could she not? He wanted to call to her, but it was too late. She had turned the corner. He wanted to run after her, but what could he say? He had accepted the lunch date with Angela. It would be impossible to explain.

Michael became agitated. He had noticed the purposeful rise in Angela's voice when Jenny walked by. He had found himself mentioning Jenny or the girls several times during the previous evening. He hadn't meant to, and he wasn't being spiteful. They were just in his thoughts. Angela mentioned that she had babysat for Jenny at various times when she was on a college break. Michael found it weird that she referred to Jenny as Mrs. Farley.

Angela must have sensed something about Michael's feelings towards Jenny. Why else would she have made a point of raising her voice and mentioning the date? Her catty attitude cleared Michael's fogged state. He would have lunch with her, and tell her that he didn't want her interfering in his life again.

By the time he reached the restaurant, he had calmed down somewhat. In the car he rehearsed what he would say to Angela. But when the time came, he played it all by ear.

They got through ordering and waiting for the meal, coasting on casual conversation. While they were eating, the time came. Angela forced him to make a decision.

"There's a great bar I know" she began "that has some pretty good groups playing on weekends. I don't usually hang out at bars. But they've got a big dance floor. I thought this weekend maybe we could go dancing together. How about it?"

Michael swallowed his bite of hamburger. "Angela ..." He paused to let out a breath. "Angela, I'm not sure how to say this. You're a nice person. But I don't think it's a good idea to go out again."

Angela remained quiet.

Michael continued. "I mean, I'm the church's intern and it might not look good to be seeing a member of the congregation."

Angela looked into his face. "That's not the truth, is it?"

Michael stammered. "W-well, i-it's a part of it. Sort of. Look, to be totally honest, I'm just not into getting involved with anyone right now. My mind's kind of occupied on other things at the moment."

"Like Mrs. Farley." she said matter-of-factly.

"She's a part of it, yes."

"When I used to babysit for her, she was always going out with different guys. She'll probably eat you up, then toss you out." Angela's words were filled with anger. "I'm just warning you. But it's your life. Do what you want."

"We're not even seeing each other right now. We've never really been on an actual date." Michael found himself explaining. "But yes, she does have a special place in my thoughts. And as long as she does, I just don't think it would be fair to you, or to me, to get involved right now."

Angela placed her napkin on the table and stood up. "I'm not really very hungry." she said quickly. "I've got to get back to work." She walked away in a fast stride.

Michael sat there, as the man at the next table stared his way. "I thought she was treating." he said to the man, who gave him a knowing nod.

Michael saw Angela in church on Sunday sitting with her family. At the end of the service, she rushed by him without speaking or shaking hands. He did not see Jenny at any of the services. His track record with women was leaving something to be desired.

At least he was still on good terms with one of the women in his life. Monday afternoon Becky stopped into his office for a visit.

"How's it going, Becky?" Michael asked casually.

"Good." she answered softly.

"How's Lisa?"

"Okay."

"How's your Mom?"

"Good."

Michael could tell she was not her usual happy self. "You look like you've got something on your mind, Becky. Want to tell me about it?"

Becky stood in the center of the room quietly thinking. "It's nothing." she finally said.

"It doesn't sound like nothing."

Becky paused again. Then she asked, "How come you don't come over to our house anymore?"

"How come?" Michael hated this aberration of the English language. But he quickly put it aside to address Becky's concern. "That's a good question. I wish I had a good answer."

"Don't you like being with us?" she asked, with pain in her voice.

"Sure I do. I'd like to come over more, but it's really up to your mother, not me."

"She's getting old you know." Becky said out of the blue. "She needs to get married before it's too late."

"Your mother is hardly what you'd call old, Becky." Michael was stunned by her frankness, but also found it humorous. "She just turned 26 less than two months ago. And 26 is not old."

"How old are you?"

Michael laughed. "It's funny you should ask. I'll be 24 on Wednesday."

"It's your birthday?" she asked excitedly, her mood suddenly changing.

"Well, in two days it will be."

"Oboy! I've gotta go." She flew out of the room and disappeared.

Michael scratched his head in bafflement of what must go on in the minds of children.

Monday and Tuesday went by without Michael giving any thought to Becky's odd behavior. He was sitting in his apartment Tuesday evening, reading, when he received a phone call.

"Hello?"

"Michael?" came the familiar voice. "This is Jenny, er, Jennifer."

Michael was silently shouting for joy; not only to hear her voice, but to hear how much of an effect he had had on her life that even she was beginning to refer to herself as Jenny. "Hello Jenny." he said happily. "I'm kind of surprised to hear from you."

"Yes, well, Beck ... Rebeccah told me it was your birthday tomorrow. She keeps talking about it. And ..., well, I was wondering if ... Did you have any plans for your birthday?"

"Not really." Michael was actually jumping up and down in his bare feet in anticipation of Jenny's next words.

"Well, if you're not doing anything, I was wondering if you'd like to do something together for your birthday."

"That would be great." He replied so fast that Jenny barely had time to finish her sentence.

"It's just that you made my birthday so special ..., well, I wanted to return the favor. What would you like for your birthday? I can make you a cake, or take you out to dinner, or you could ..."

"You know what would really make me happy?" Michael said, cutting her off.

"What's that?"

"What I'd really like for my birthday is to spend some time with you. Just the two of us together. That would really make my birthday special for me."

The line was quiet for a while. "Well, all right." Jenny finally said. "I'm working the day shift tomorrow. But I'm free for dinner."

"Why don't you come over here?" Michael suggested. "I'll make us dinner."

"All right. What time?"

"Whenever you can make it."

"Six o'clock. Is that all right?"

"I'll see you then."

"All right. Goodbye, Michael."

"Good night, Jenny. Thanks." He hung up the receiver and began dancing around the living room floor.

It was five minutes to six. He looked around, making a last minute inspection of the apartment. There wasn't much to check. The furnishing was sparse, with a couch, side table, chair, lamp, and small dining table, none of it matching, all of it used furniture donated by different members of the congregation. It made him feel like he was living in a Salvation Army drop-off station. But it wasn't so bad. He wasn't there that much. And for his first real place of his own, it was kind of nice. Everything seemed to be in order.

It was now a few minutes past six. He wasn't expecting her to be on time. He checked on the dinner. He had prepared a real meal, something he had never done before. The corn and steak was easy. The baked potatoes were no problem. The hardest thing to prepare was the salad. He had never eaten a salad before, so he wasn't sure what went into one. That morning he had purchased several different varieties of lettuce. Until that day he had never realized there was more than one kind of lettuce. He also selected six different bottles of salad dressing from the endless variety taking up an entire store shelf. He didn't know what else to put in the salad, so he added some tomato slices to it. He was pretty sure that it was edible, but it looked a real mess. He tore the heads of lettuce to shreds with his hands. The next time, maybe he should try a knife, he thought to himself.

The intercom buzzer sounded at twelve after six. He was expecting her to be even later. He buzzed her in.

"You're early." he said, as she entered into the living room.

"What?"

"Nothing. Just a joke. Here, I'll take your coat."

She was wearing a long, down-filled, tan coat which made her look puffy. She took it off and handed it to Michael. He placed it on the couch. Jenny was wearing tan cowboy boots with brown gaucho pants. Michael had never even heard the term 'gaucho' before meeting Jenny. She had flesh colored stockings which sparkled. Her off-white sweater also had sparkles in it. She looked beautiful.

They stood awkwardly for a few moments in the center of the living room. Finally, Jenny offered him the brown paper bag she was holding.

"Happy Birthday, Michael." she said.

"Should I open this?" He wasn't expecting a gift. He never knew what to do with presents when he got them.

"That's what it's for."

They sat on the couch as Michael opened the bag. Inside, there was a wrapped present with a large homemade card on it made out of light blue construction paper. The cover of the card had 'Happy Birthday' printed on it in different crayon colors. He could tell a child had done it. He opened up the card. Inside was drawn several different colored balloons and what Michael guessed was a birthday cake with five black candles on it. Both Becky's and Lisa's names were printed on it, done by their own hand. By their names was the message 'With Love' with a big red heart drawn beside it.

"This is great, really great." he said a number of times in all sincerity.

"It was Becky's idea. But they both worked on it. They spent a lot of time on it too. That's the second one. They messed up the first one."

"Well it's really great." he said again. "Just great."

He had never had a present move him in such a warm way before. He felt like they were almost his own children.

"Should I open the present now?" He felt stupid asking.

"It's for you. You might as well."

"Okay."

He knew what it was before he even opened it. The package was so thin and flexible it could only be a calendar. He already had several calendars for the new year. It seemed all the funeral homes in the area sent calendars to the local ministers. But he was pleasantly surprised when he opened it to see what kind of calendar it was.

"The Beatles!" he exclaimed, like a little child at Christmas. "How did you know?"

"I remember you mentioning once how much you liked The Beatles. When I saw the calendar in the card shop, I knew it was the perfect gift for you."

"It is. It is." he found himself repeating again.

He loved the calendar. But what made it all the more special for him was that Jenny remembered something mentioned in passing months earlier. She was listening. Maybe she was interested in him even back then. The calendar was a good sign. It was a sign of hope for Michael.

Again, a long moment of awkward silence followed. Neither knew what step to take next. The bell chime on the oven timer provided the next step.

"The potatoes are ready." he said, getting up. "Let me just check on everything else and I think we'll be ready to eat in just a few minutes."

He took the potatoes out of the oven and placed the steak, which he had already broiled, back in to heat up. The corn was keeping warm on the stove.

"Can I help with anything?" Jenny said, stepping toward the kitchen area.

"No, we're all set. Have a seat." He motioned towards the tiny dining table.

As she sat down, he placed the collection of salad dressings on the table in front of her.

"I wasn't sure which kind you liked." he said sheepishly. He placed the bowl of salad on the table. "We can start with the salad while the steak's getting ready." he said, sitting.

"It's your birthday and you're cooking for me." she said in wonder. "I should have had you over for dinner."

"That's all right. I wanted to do this. You can invite me over another time. Did you want something to drink?"

"A glass of red wine would be nice."

"Oh, I don't have any wine." he said, perturbed with himself for not thinking of getting wine.

"I forgot, you don't drink wine." she said.

"I have soda." he offered.

"That's all right. I don't drink soda."

"I forgot." He felt stupid.

It felt like they were going back in time, starting from the beginning.

"I'll just have coffee later." she said nicely.

"Oh." He couldn't believe he had forgotten to buy coffee as well. "I don't have any coffee."

"You don't drink coffee either. I forgot. Oh well, there's always your favorite - water." She began placing salad on her plate as he got two glasses of water.

Dinner seemed to go well. She commented several times on how she couldn't believe he had cooked dinner for her. "No one has ever done that for me before." she kept saying. She seemed to enjoy the meal well enough. At least, she ate the whole meal on only one glass of water. That was a good sign.

Michael cleared the table as Jenny sat there. He refused her offer of help.

"Oh, I didn't get you a cake." she suddenly blurted out.

"That's okay. I got one." He pulled a box out of the refrigerator. "I didn't feel like making one, so I bought one at the store."

It was a chocolate cake with vanilla frosting. They both had a big piece. Michael was impressed that Jenny was not one of those women who asked for only a tiny piece, and then ended up sticking their fork into yours to have more. After dessert, they went back to sit on the couch. Michael lit the one candle that he had, but left the living room light on. He turned on his small portable radio that was on the table holding the lamp. The radio station was playing mostly Christmas music.

"I notice you don't have any Christmas decorations up yet." Jenny said, observing the room around her.

"Yeah, well I really didn't bring any with me. And what's the point of buying any. It's just me. You're the only person that's ever been over here."

"Not even Angela?" she said, too quietly to make out clearly.

"What?"

"Never mind. You're not even going to get a tree?" she said quickly to change the subject.

"I thought about it. I was going to, but it seemed a waste just for me." Michael tilted his head back on the couch, remembering Christmases past. "That was always my favorite thing about Christmas, even better than the presents. I loved decorating the tree for Christmas, and then looking at all the lights blinking on the tree. I'd turn out all the house lights and just stare at the tree lights. They made neat patterns on the ceiling as they blinked on and off." Michael sat back up. "But the best part of all was going to get the tree with my family. To me, that signaled that the Christmas season had begun. And we had the most fun times doing it. It was one of the few times that I remember that we were really a family." Michael seemed to be getting lost in his thoughts.

"You have brothers and sisters?" Jenny asked, trying to bring him back.

"Just an older sister, Julie. We used to rush to find the perfect tree. I'd pick one and she'd pick another. Then my parents had to choose between the two. My father always liked Julie's the best. My mother always picked mine. We usually always ended up getting Julie's tree. But every once in a while, my mother would convince my father to let us get my tree. Then Julie would throw a royal fit in the car all the way home. My, those were good times."

The next silence lasted through the radio's playing of 'O Tannenbaum'.

"Can I ask you a favor?" Michael said, almost jumping off the couch. "Did you get your Christmas tree yet?"

"No, we usually wait until the week before Christmas."

"Can I go with you?"

"I suppose. But I usually just go out myself at night and pick one up at a place near the diner."

"Oh, but we've all got to go. We've got to take the kids. Can we?" He felt like a small child, begging his mother.

"I guess. We could go Monday afternoon after Becky's swimming lesson at the Y."

"Terrific." Michael was happy that this evening would not end being the last time he would be seeing Jenny. Tomorrow was looking up.

He drove over from the church to the YWCA. It didn't take him long to find Jenny and Lisa sitting on a bench by the side of the pool. He joined them.

"Hi. Where's Becky?"

"She's in the water." Lisa answered. "Right there." she said, pointing.

"Okay, I see her." Michael didn't really see her. All the girls in the pool looked the same to him with their hair pulled up inside white bathing caps.

"She'll be done soon." Jenny said. "How was work today?"

"Same old thing. Nobody new in the hospital. I have to do a funeral for Eric on Thursday, though."

"Who died?"

"Someone named Willy Vanderslice."

"I don't recognize that name."

"Karen said he's a C & E member, Christmas and Easter."

"Here comes Rebeccah." Lisa announced.

"Hi Mommy." Becky was dripping water all over Jenny. But Jenny didn't seem to mind. "Did you see me swimming?"

"I sure did. You were doing great. I think we've got a future Olympic gold medalist in the making."

"Cut it out, Mom." Becky smiled through her protest.

"Go get changed so we can get our tree."

"Okay. I'll be right back."

About twenty minutes later, Becky finally emerged from the girls' locker room. They were on their way.

"Why don't we take my car?" Michael suggested when they came out to the parking lot. "It's a little larger than yours."

They all got into Michael's car and drove to a lot selling Christmas trees. Unlike when he and his sister were kids, Michael noted that the girls stuck close by their mother instead of running off to find the perfect tree. It was clear to him that he would have to take the lead.

"All right, everybody. Be on the lookout for the perfect tree."

"How do we know which is the best one?" Becky asked.

"You'll just know. You can feel it."

"How about that one?" Lisa pointed to a small tree in front of her.

"No, too puny. We can do better. Let's keep trying."

They pulled a number of trees out and stood them up for evaluation. Some weren't full enough, others weren't tall enough. The girls kept pointing. Finally, Lisa found a winner.

"Now this is a tree." Michael said, admiringly. "I think we've found the one. What do you think?"

Both Lisa and Becky chimed in, "Yeah."

Michael felt like his own father. He was basking in the family mood - until he saw how much the perfect tree cost. But he insisted on paying for it despite Jenny's protests. Since he was the one who had invited himself along, since it was his tradition they were reliving, it was only fair that he should pay for the tree. He just hadn't banked on the high price that came with playing the father role. As an intern, he was living on a small monthly stipend that the church provided him.

One piece of the family tradition that Michael had overlooked was that his family always had a big station wagon to fit the tree into. Michael's old Chevrolet Impala was not exactly tree sized. As he deliberated over a way to fit the tree into the back seat, Jenny explained that she always took a piece of rope to tie the tree into the trunk. Since he didn't have any rope with him, he did not find the suggestion helpful.

Through much struggling, he finally managed to pull the tree into the car so that the bottom end filled the back seat, while the top of the tree took up part of the front passenger seat as it extended out the front window.

"Well, that'll do it." Michael said, breathing hard.

"Oh, it's perfect, all right." Jenny said, sarcastically. "Now tell me, where should we sit?"

He felt like crying. Traditions always seemed easier from the eyes of youth.

With a little repositioning, he managed to fit Becky into the back seat, though the tree quickly engulfed her. Jenny sat uncomfortably in the front, clutching Lisa on her lap, with the tree sticking into her side. Fortunately, it was a short drive back to the YWCA parking lot. Michael could only take so much of Jenny muttering under her breath just how dangerous driving like this was.

Back at Jenny's house, getting the tree out of the car proved more difficult than getting it in. By the time he got it out, the tree was considerably less full than it had been at the tree lot. Pine needles littered the back seat of his car. More pine needles fell off as he tried to fit the tree through Jenny's front door. Michael stood the tree up in the living room by the bay window. It just cleared the ceiling. Perfect, he thought. Then Jenny brought out the stand with the decorations. Michael set the tree down to attach the stand. When he tried to put the tree back upright, he found that the top now bent back against the ceiling. He almost swore, but then noticed Lisa standing beside him looking toward the ceiling.

"It's too big." she observed.

"You noticed." Michael said dryly.

He set the tree back down and took off the stand. Jenny got him a saw from the garage, and he proceeded to cut off part of the base.

Setting the tree back up on its stand, he found that once again it just cleared the ceiling.

"Finally." he muttered.

"I'm going to start dinner." Jenny said. "Are you staying?"

"Sure, if I'm invited." he replied, his mood suddenly picking up.

"Why don't you three start putting on the decorations while I'm making dinner. Chicken okay?"

"Great." He was relieved it was not quiche.

Michael untangled the set of lights with Becky's assistance, while Lisa waited impatiently to start putting on her favorite ornaments. By the time dinner was ready, the tree was decorated.

"I'm glad that's over with." he said with a sigh. It was fun, but more work than he had anticipated. "I'm starving. Let's eat."

"Wait." Lisa said. "We have to put up the angel."

"Angel? What angel?"

"The angel that always goes on top of the tree." she said, pulling one last decoration from the box.

Michael looked up at the top of the tree. There was no room to place an angel on top. And there was no way that he was about to take off all the ornaments to cut the base down more.

"Do we really need the angel this year?" he said helplessly.

"We always have the angel." Lisa said definitively.

He looked towards Becky for help.

"She's right. We always have the angel." she concurred.

He looked at Jenny for support.

"What can I say? We always have the angel."

With defeat in his voice, Michael answered, "Okay. You all have dinner. I'll figure something out."

After rearranging some of the lights and ornaments that sat toward the top of the tree, he cut off some of the top branches to make room for the angel. Satisfied that the tree was now complete, he joined the others for dinner just as they were clearing the table.

"I saved you some dinner." Jenny said sweetly. "It's in the oven keeping warm. The tree looks great."

Jenny's nurturing voice made all the struggle worthwhile. Michael was feeling good about the way everything was taking shape.

The rest of the evening advanced nicely. After the children were safely tucked in for the night, Jenny and Michael retreated to the couch for some relaxed conversation. This time, instead of candlelight, they relied on the Christmas lights to set the appropriate mood. Talk came so easily and so freely that it seemed like there had never been an interruption in their relationship. The almost two months of separation and pain Michael had endured washed away in the gentle glow of Jenny's presence.

After a while, the talking stopped. They stared at the lights of the tree and listened to Christmas music on the stereo. Michael looked over at Jenny. She was asleep. All was right with the world. He sat for a while, alternating his gaze from the tree to Jenny. If ever there was a moment he wished to capture for all time, this was it. He felt incredibly at peace. He was very reluctant to move at all, let alone leave. But he knew that tomorrow would not put itself on hold for him, and there was much work waiting to greet him with the new day. The Christmas season was an extremely busy time in the life of the congregation. He needed to get some sleep.

He slowly got up and turned out the Christmas tree lights after turning on the living room light. Then he turned the stereo off and made his exit, having perfected the art of locking the front door without making any noise.

❖❖❖

The week before Christmas Michael did not see much of Jenny. But this time it was due to his own busy schedule. He did manage to talk to her on the phone each night before going to bed. It was nice to maintain this connection, but it was not the same as spending time together. Michael viewed every moment not spent with Jenny as an opportunity forever lost to time. But she stayed in his thoughts as he went about his work. He hoped that he was in hers as well.

An indication that Michael's hopes were possibly being fulfilled came in their phone conversation on December 22. They had been talking about the different Christmas services being held at the church. Jenny would be attending the early evening Family Service Christmas Eve with her children. Michael was preparing a special children's sermon for the service. Eric was also letting him preach at the midnight Candlelight Service, and he shared with Jenny how nervous he was about it.

"I'm sorry I won't be there to hear you." she apologized, after reassuring him that it would all go well. "But it's hard enough to get the girls to go to sleep on Christmas Eve without getting home after midnight." Jenny hesitated for a moment, then asked, "Listen, would you like to come over following the late service for some Christmas refreshments? I thought it might be nice to share some of the holiday together, unless you have other plans."

Michael was at once elated and crushed. He was overjoyed that she wanted to be with him for Christmas, but he did have other plans. He promised his father and stepmother that he would come home for Christmas morning. They really wanted him home Christmas Eve, and were very disappointed that his work would prevent him from being there. His sister Julie would be at the house with her husband, Roger, which meant their children, Ryan and Julia, would be looking forward to the arrival of their favorite uncle. He couldn't disappoint the family. He was planning on heading out for Lancaster immediately after the midnight service -which actually began at 11 p.m. and ended at midnight - was over. That way, he would have a few hours' sleep at his parents' home before being awoken by his niece and nephew Christmas morning. He did want to be there to watch them open their presents. As much as he would have liked to spend a piece of Christmas with Jenny, he would have to tell her he couldn't come.

"Come over after the service?" he gulped. "That sounds really nice. Sure, I can come."

"Good." she said. "I'll make something special. So I guess I'll see you Christmas Eve then."

"I'm looking forward to it."

"Goodnight, Michael."

"Bye."

After hanging up the receiver, he did some quick recalculating in his head. He could stay at Jenny's for a couple of hours, then head for home, forego sleep, and still make it back in time for the opening of presents. Giving up sleep was no sacrifice at all in exchange for the opportunity of spending some quality time with Jenny. He went to sleep happy. This would be the best Christmas since he was a little kid and he received the electric wood-carving set he always wanted.

Michael's head was a jumble throughout the day of Christmas Eve. He had the services to worry about, and his two sermons. But weighing more heavily on his mind was the fact that in all the time spent with Jenny, they had never even touched, let alone been intimate. They were growing closer, but had never kissed or even held hands. Michael was determined to change all that. Christmas was the opportunity he needed to make a forward step.

It wasn't that he was shy or inexperienced. He had dated plenty of girls before without a problem. But they were girls. Jenny was a woman. He wasn't in high school or college any longer. He was moving toward an adult relationship, one that had met with some resistance and unclear signals. He was afraid of being rejected once again. But he couldn't tread water forever. Something had to happen to let Jenny know how he felt, and to discover how she felt in return. Maybe she had some mistletoe in the house. No, he knew that she didn't. It would be beyond tacky to bring some himself. Well, there was nothing wrong with sharing a goodnight kiss in the spirit of Christmas good cheer, was there? That was it. Whatever the consequences, he was determined to give her a kiss before leaving her house. For someone entering into an adult relationship, he sure felt like a little kid all over again.

CHAPTER SIX

now

He sat nervously, looking around the office, as the man across the desk studied the document Michael had handed him. It seemed to be taking forever. He glanced at the wall containing framed degrees. It gave him a little confidence that this man was a legitimate lawyer. He studied the name plate on the desk – 'Walter Boelhower, Esq'. Michael tried to figure out this man holding his fate in his hands without appearing to be staring at him. He looked older than his brother-in-law, Roger, even though he knew the two had been college roommates. Maybe it was the balding head that made him appear older. Finally, the man put the papers down and addressed Michael.

"Well, I see what's happening here, Mr. Griggs." Mr. Boelhower said, matter-of-factly. "First off, you misunderstood what's being demanded in this court order. Which is understandable, as you are not a lawyer. They like to throw a lot of legal language in these things so as to make it as obtuse as possible, making it virtually impossible for the layman to know what's being said."

Mr. Boelhower smiled to put Michael at ease. But he could see that Michael was too wound up to be comfortable, so he continued.

"The demanding party is not seeking custody directly. They're seeking visitation rights."

"I'm not sure I understand." Michael sat forward in his chair.

"The plaintiffs are … Wait, let me start over. What this boils down to is that the grandparents of your two little … girls? Girls, yes. The grandparents want visitation rights. They want to see … What are the little girls' names?"

"Becky and Lisa."

"Becky and Lisa. Well, the grandparents have been granted a court order to see Becky and Lisa, under court supervision, with the intent of establishing permanent visitation rights, and leaving open the possibility of seeking some form of custody in the future, dependent on the outcome of the visits, and certain criteria being met."

"I think I understood you up to that last part." Michael was fidgeting nervously.

"Well, let's just say for now it's not as bad as you thought it was. They're not trying to take the girls away. At least not for now. For now, they've been granted the right to be a part of the girls' lives, giving them supervised visiting rights."

"Can they do that?"

"Well, again, as I told you when you first came in, this is not my area of law. I'm a Patent Attorney. But I have heard of this. There are recognized precedents for Grandparents' Rights. So they do have a case."

"So if I let them see the girls, what then?"

"Well, first off, you have to let them see the girls. That's what this Court Order means. You have no choice in the matter. But the best I can determine from this is that the Judge granting the order will be following up on the case and can consider giving the grandparents temporary or even permanent custody if she decides it's warranted."

"Warranted? What does that mean?"

"Well, again, this is not really my field of expertise, but from what I can gather there will be a field person assigned to this case who will be acting as the Judge's eyes and ears. And that person could recommend giving the grandparents custody if they think it's in the best interests of the children."

"I can't believe they can do that. This is so unreal. There must be something we can do."

"I'm sure there is. This is not a done deal by any means. But let me ask you, did your late wife leave a will or any legal document naming you guardian?"

"No." Michael's heart sank at the question.

"Well, that does make it a little messier. But not insurmountable. Listen, let me do some research. I'll talk to a colleague in the firm who might be more up to speed on this kind of thing. I can also contact the grandparents' lawyer and get some more information."

"Can you do that?"

"Sure. The contact information is in with the document. It's no big thing to make a simple phone call. Maybe something can be worked out without having to resort to a long protracted legal battle. That serves no one in this case."

"Thank you, Mr. Boelhower." Michael stood up to shake his hand. "You have no idea how much I appreciate your help."

"Don't mention it, son. Your brother-in-law and I go way back. I'm happy to help out a friend. Let me do some research and I'll get back to you."

"Thank you again, sir." Michael started to leave, but was stopped by the attorney.

"One more thing, Mr. Griggs."

"Yes?"

"I understand right now that you're unemployed."

"Well, sort of. That is, I'm starting up a furniture business."

"Starting up? I see. Let me just say, as a word of friendly advice, having a steady job with a steady income will be a definite factor in any decision made about the girls' future. I strongly suggest you give that some serious thought."

"I will, sir. Thank you again."

Michael walked out of the office with a whole new problem to deal with.

Michael found himself sitting on some boxes in the garage. He had come in to do some more cleaning up, while deciding if he could make a go of this furniture business. But the thought of possibly losing custody of the girls was overwhelming him. He couldn't do any work. Instead, he looked around the garage, trying to rein in his wandering thoughts. There was no way he could get a new business started now. But what could he do? There was only one realistic option. But he couldn't bring himself to accept it. His faith was gone. It would be hypocritical to consider going back into the ministry. He tried to push the thought out of his head. But it wouldn't leave. At the same time, he couldn't let it become a reality. Too much pain stood in the way. He was at an impasse. That's when he heard the front doorbell.

Surprise, bordering on shock, came over his face as he opened the door to see his old mentor, Eric Nordtveit, standing there. He hadn't seen him since the wedding. He found himself harboring resentment toward Eric for being away when Jenny died and not doing the funeral service. He understood the reasons, but the resentment hung in there just the same. He hesitated in inviting Eric inside. But routine courtesy won the day. Eric came inside and took a seat on the couch.

Not surprisingly, words of apology were the first things out of Eric's mouth.

"Mike, I'm so sorry about not being there for you and Jennifer. As you know, I've been away on sabbatical in Israel for the past several months. I tried calling several times. I hope you got the messages."

Michael nodded. He had gotten the messages, but chose to ignore them.

"I've been thinking about you so much." Eric continued. "You know how much Jennifer meant to me. She was such a welcome addition to our church family. I thought of her as one of my own daughters. It was so sad to lose her at such a young age. I am really sorry that I couldn't be there for her toward the end. I truly wish I could have been there to do the service for her. But I know Pastor Jones. He's a good man, a real man of God. Even though he's been retired for several years, he still puts a lot of care into what he does. How did the service go?"

"It went." Michael responded coldly.

"Well, anyway," Eric plowed through, "how are the girls doing?"

"They're doing about as well as can be expected under the circumstances." Michael shifted slightly in his chair, waiting for the next inevitable question.

"And how about you? How are you doing? I'm sure it's been a trying time."

"You could say that." Michael stopped, not sure if he should say anything else or keep quiet and put a quick end to this uncomfortable meeting. But he felt the need to continue. "It hasn't been easy."

"I'm sure it hasn't."

"Truthfully, I've been having a lot of sleepless nights. And I find myself floundering around like I'm in a perpetual fog. I'm drifting through life, Eric, and I don't know what to do."

Eric did not respond. Michael could see that he was taking in his words, waiting for him to continue. And Michael found himself wanting to continue. He was quickly letting go of his resentment toward Eric, which he always knew was irrational. Standing face to face with his mentor now, all he saw was the role model and surrogate father figure that he had come to rely upon.

"Eric, something's just happened. It's a real mess and I don't know what to do about it."

"What is it, Mike? What's happened?"

"I got these papers, court papers. They were from Jenny's ex-husband's parents. They want to see Becky and Lisa."

"Well, that's not so bad, is it? Having grandparents in the picture can be a good thing. But Jennifer never talked much about her ex-husband. Have these grandparents been around the girls that much?"

"No. They've never even met. They've just popped up out of nowhere. And there's the possibility that they could take the girls away from me."

"No, Mike. That doesn't seem likely."

"But it can happen. I've seen a lawyer. These strangers can move to seek custody if they want to. And they could win." Michael got up and began pacing uncontrollably. "They're blood relatives. I'm just one guy who hasn't a clue what he's doing. What business do I have in trying to raise two little girls? I'm probably doing them more damage than good."

"Mike, I understand you being upset and doubting yourself. But you've got to put those doubts aside and know that you're doing a good job. Jennifer would want the girls to be with you. She wouldn't have married you if she didn't think you were good for her daughters. They were the most important things in her life."

"Yeah, you're right." Michael calmed down and sat back in the chair. "I know you're right. As bad as things have gotten, I still see Jenny's face every night telling me to take care of Lisa and Becky. It's just all so scary right now."

"What's the scariest part for you?"

"Just thinking that I could lose Becky and Lisa. I couldn't live with that. They're all I have left of Jenny. I'm always seeing her in everything they do."

Eric got up from the couch and stood beside Michael, placing his arm on Michael's shoulder.

"If that's what scares you the most, it just shows how important those two little girls are to you. Which means that you're going to do everything in your power to make sure they stay with you. You've got the will to fight for them. And that's going to be in your favor."

"Eric, there's something else." Michael hesitated.

"What is it, Mike? Tell me."

"In order to have a chance at keeping the girls, I need to have a job, a steady source of income."

"Well, there's one obvious solution to that and I'm sure you know what it is. So what's the hesitation?" Eric sat back down on the couch, this time sitting closer to Michael.

"How can I be a minister when I don't believe in God?"

Eric took a moment to absorb Michael's words.

"Is it that you don't believe in God or more that you're angry at God?"

"I was angry. But now it just feels numb. Does that make sense?"

"I think so. But tell me more."

"I'm not angry at God. I can't see a real being to be angry at. I used to see God, or what I perceived as God, very clearly. Now I don't see anything. It's just a blank space where my faith used to be. Any feelings I used to have when it comes to there being a God have been replaced by this numbness. I can't evoke any feelings toward a Supreme Being at all. It's a black hole."

"Mike, Michael, I won't pretend to know what you're going through right now. I can just say that the Michael I came to know was a man who had what I would call a quiet faith. You didn't talk about it that much, but it was obviously there. God just seemed to be there with you wherever you went. It showed in everything you said and in everything you did. Maybe that presence has grown silent right now, but I think, I hope, it's still there. My faith tells me God is still there. He's just waiting for you to re-discover his presence."

"I don't know, Eric. Yeah, there was something that I always felt was there as long as I could remember. But it's gone. It's absolutely gone. I know that."

The two sat in silence for what seemed an eternity.

"So what then?" Eric asked. "Where do you go from here?"

"I don't know. I honestly don't know. That's what's got me so messed up right now. I'm lost."

"Let me throw out a scenario for a moment." Eric offered.

"Go ahead. What are you thinking?"

"Let's consider for a moment the fact that you need a job of some sort. You could possibly find something, but let's face facts. It's unlikely you could find something quickly that would be both satisfying and pay well. You need a job with some standing in the community that would impress a judge. Something that's more of a career than a job. Something with some flexible hours so you could be there for the girls as well."

"I know where you're going with this, Eric, but ..."

"Bear with me a bit longer here, Mike. You put in four years of your life studying for the ministry. Why throw that all away?"

"Because I don't believe in God."

"I know. I know. And I'm not trying to brush that aside. Believe me, Michael, if I truly believed that there was no chance for you to get back your faith, I wouldn't be advocating for this. Being a minister is definitely not for everybody. And it certainly isn't for someone who is not walking humbly with God. But that's not you, Michael. I just know it isn't. I respect where you are in your journey right now. But I believe that for you it's just a temporary detour from what has been your entire faith journey through life. God is still there – beside you and inside you. You will find your way back to Him. I am confident of this."

"I'm glad you are, but ..."

"All right, let me put it this way. You've already come this far in becoming a minister. Why not go a little further in the process? Maybe if you start moving forward, you might find your faith coming back. And if it doesn't, you can always bow out of the process before it's too late, just like you did before. What have you got to lose?"

"Well ..."

"Michael ..."

"Yeah?"

"I honestly and sincerely believe that the possibility of what you might find will make this all worthwhile."

"You might be right, Eric. But it's probably too late already. I really burnt a bridge when I backed out of the process the first time. I doubt they'll give me another chance."

"You let me take care of that. The Chairperson of the Candidacy Committee was one of my first interns. She owes me a favor. Say the word and I'll talk to her today."

"I don't know. Maybe. Give me one night to think about it, at least."

"One night. You got it. I'll call you tomorrow." Eric almost jumped out of his seat and moved toward the door before Michael could change his mind.

Just as Michael was about to close the door, Eric turned around and added, "But you know, I was just thinking. It couldn't hurt if I called her today just to feel her out. You can still say no. But this way, you'll know where the Committee's thinking is at. How about it?"

"Sure, go ahead." Michael responded resignedly. "I need to get moving on this."

"Great! Call you tomorrow. And Mike?"

"Yeah."

"I'm praying for you." With that, Eric beat a hasty retreat.

CHAPTER SEVEN

now

Once the girls were safely on their way to school, Michael headed out for his appointment at the lawyer's office. He found concentrating on the road difficult. His mind was a jumble of questions. What did the lawyer find out? How would he respond to Eric's phone call, if indeed Eric did call back? Did he have the guts to face the Synod Candidacy Committee? What could he possibly say to them? Was there any other alternative? What if he lost the girls? That was the question that kept coming back into his thoughts. It was the one question whose answer he couldn't face.

He jammed on the brakes, barely stopping in time at the red light. The sudden jolt brought his attention back to his driving. He was almost at the lawyer's office. He had been driving for twenty minutes on auto pilot.

He couldn't wait for the pleasantries to be over with so that he could find out what his lawyer had to say. Finally, Mr. Boelhower had him take a seat.

"Well, Michael, I have some good news and some not so good news. What would you like to hear first?" Mr. Boelhower melted back into his plush leather chair at his desk.

"I want to hear all of it." Michael was almost rising out of his own stiff cloth chair looking out onto the oversized desk facing him. "Please tell me what you've found out."

"Well, yes, certainly." Mr. Boelhower shifted nervously in his seat. "I contacted the lawyer representing the grandparents. Nice fellow. We attended the same law school it turns out. Different years, of course. He was several years behind me. We did have a lot of the same law professors, however."

"Mr. Boelhower, please. I'm dying here."

"What? Oh yes. I'm sorry. Excuse my babbling. Okay, so here's what I know so far." He tipped his glasses slightly down his nose and looked at a yellow legal pad on his desk. "Mr. and Mrs. Farley are the parents of John Farley, the biological father of ..." He paused to take a closer look at his notes. " ...Rebeccah and Lisa Farley. They are the ones petitioning for custody of the girls."

"Yes, I know. We've established all this already." Michael's impatience was evident.

"Yes, yes. True enough. But did you know that the father, John Farley, is dead?"

"What!? No, I didn't know that. Jenny never had contact with him again after he left."

"Well now, you see!" Mr. Boelhower seemed pleased with himself that he was able to offer some new information. But sensing Michael's anxiety, he quickly reeled himself in. "Yes, he died in a motorcycle crash earlier this year. He was speeding, weaving in and out of traffic and ... Well, the details don't matter. What's important is that the Farley's, the parents, were going through his things after his death and discovered an old letter which mentioned his daughters. They had never known that they were grandparents. He had never told them about the girls."

"Not surprising, from what Jenny told me about him. But that should work in my favor, though, right? I mean, it shows that he never had any interest in the girls at all."

"Yes, I see your point. But no, it doesn't help your case. It helps the Farley's in explaining why they never had previous contact with their grandchildren. They didn't know. They were unfairly denied that knowledge."

"Yeah, I can see why that's not good. But it was hardly my fault. Why should I get punished for their ignorance?"

"Why should the Farley's be punished? And why should the girls be punished by not knowing their grandparents?"

"Whose lawyer are you, anyway?" Michael instantly regretted his harsh tone.

"I'm sorry, Michael. I know this must be hard for you. What the Farley's are seeking is the chance to get to know their grandchildren. The court has already granted them provisional visiting rights under court appointed supervision. That's Step One."

"What's Step Two?"

"If things go well, the Farley's have been granted the right to seek some sort of custody, either a joint custody arrangement, or, if the court deems it appropriate, full custodial rights."

Michael got up and started pacing, while Mr. Boelhower continued to sit in comfort.

"I just don't understand it. This makes no sense. How could any court do this?"

"The big problem here, Michael, is that Jennifer never sat down with a lawyer to make any provision for the children in the case of her death. The Farley's are the girls' closest living blood relatives. You're not. I'm sorry."

Mr. Boelhower allowed Michael to pace until he was worn out. When Michael finally sat down, he continued.

"Look, son, it's not all bad news. Yes, court decisions have set a precedent for Grandparents' Rights. But the courts have also traditionally weighed favorably on the side of the person who already has the established relationship with the child. Or children in this case."

"Well, I guess that's something. Isn't it?"

"Yes, it is! But look, like I told you before, you have a lot of work to do to show that you can support the children. I'm not going to lie. Not having a steady job is going to hurt you. Have you done anything to resolve that issue?"

"Yeah, I have someone working on that for me right now. Hopefully, I'll hear something before the end of the day."

"That's good, Michael. Very good. Very important. I can't stress that enough. You need to show that you're providing a stable environment for the children."

"I get it. So what's next?"

"I've made arrangement with the Farley's attorney to set up their first supervised visit. It's this weekend. They'll be staying at a nearby hotel and coming Saturday morning to pick up the girls."

"This weekend? So soon? Will I be able to go with them?"

"No. You must not interfere in any way. There will be a woman from Social Services with them who will be with them at all times. She'll ensure their safety, while also studying the interaction for further recommendations. There will also be another person from Social Services meeting with you. She'll be contacting you this week to set up an initial appointment. Be as accommodating as possible. You need to put your best foot forward. She'll also be making recommendations based on your interview and future observed interactions with the girls."

"This is all becoming too real."

"It is real, Michael. As real as it gets."

CHAPTER EIGHT

now

Eric's phone call came that afternoon. He was relieved that Eric had come through, but also shaken that things were moving so quickly. The Candidacy Committee had agreed to meet with him. At first, they wanted to schedule the meeting for some time in the new year, but Eric called in a few favors and convinced the committee members to call a special meeting the following week - on October 31.

"Why does that date sound familiar?" Michael thought to himself. "Of course. It's the date for Reformation, the date Martin Luther posted the 95 Theses."

Now that he had that sorted out, he quickly let it slip out of his mind as he concentrated on what he would say to the Committee. They were the ones who would decide his fate - again. The same people had met with him throughout his years in seminary. They had approved him as a candidate to receive a call to a parish. Without that approval, his years of seminary would have been for nothing. They alone had the power to say 'Yea' or 'Nay' to his becoming a pastor.

Except he had taken that power away from them. They approved him, but he rejected their approval. He walked away from it all after four years of hard work and study. They couldn't have been too pleased with him. If it hadn't been for Eric's intervention, the door would have been closed, most likely slammed in his face. Instead, at the Bishop's recommendation, thanks to a phone call from Eric, the Committee placed him on the 'On Leave from Call' list, a list of pastors without a call to a congregation. It meant that Michael could have his status as a minister reactivated, at the Committee's discretion. It was going to be an uphill battle.

As much as it pained him to think about the upcoming meeting with the Candidacy Committee, there was another thought intruding on his mind that pained him even more – he had to find a way to tell the girls that they were about to meet their grandparents.

CHAPTER NINE

then

The true wonder of the early Christmas Eve service, with the beautiful carols, the Nativity story, and Eric's inspirational message, managed to take his mind off his own interests so that he was able to feel the genuine spirit of Christmas and appreciate the true meaning of the celebration. He did see Jenny at the end of the service, but she was just a sweet, nice moment in an awe inspiring evening. Michael did take notice that she was wearing a long red dress with a short, black velvet dress jacket. He thought it looked nice. But then his mind was quickly refocused onto the midnight service and his own sermon to come.

The late service was even more moving, especially when the parishioners sang 'Silent Night', bathed in the warm glow of candlelight. It was about twenty minutes past midnight by the time Michael finished shaking hands with everyone at the door and exchanging greetings of 'Merry Christmas'. He received a few favorable comments on his sermon. One of the members gave him a jar of homemade preserves as a Christmas gift. Then everyone was gone, off to their own homes and families. Michael stood alone in the darkened church. It left him a little sad. It was a magical evening of communal sharing. But then the community split up to return to their own lives. It was a shame the moment could not last a little longer.

But he quickly remembered that he had somewhere to go. His sense of isolation was only temporary. He had someone to share with and extend the moment. He was dead tired from the long evening's work, but also renewed by having a place and a person to go to. He quickly locked up the doors and headed out.

There was a light snow beginning to fall as Michael walked to his car. It lightened the sky so that it felt more like daybreak than the deep of the night. The windshield wipers clearing the snow away from his windshield had a hypnotic effect as he drove along the deserted road. He felt himself nodding off. He tried to find a good Rock 'n Roll song on the radio to revive him, but all he could find being broadcast were Catholic Midnight Masses.

Everything looked dark as he pulled up to Jenny's house. He wondered if Jenny had forgotten, and gone to bed. Panic seized him for a moment. Maybe she just fell asleep on the couch again waiting for him. Anxiously, he knocked quietly on the front door. Jenny soon appeared at the door.

Michael was taken aback, stunned by the sight before him. Jenny was wearing the same red dress she had on at church, but it looked so much different now. She had removed the black jacket, revealing a sleeveless, low-cut gown, held up ever so gently by two string-size straps. The silken material of the dress clung tightly to her curvaceous form. As the soft candlelight behind her framed her beauty, Michael swore that he had never seen a sexier sight in his entire life. His mind went blank as his leering eyes took over.

Before he could take a step, before he could say anything, before his mind could begin functioning again, Jenny gave him an affectionate kiss on the lips.

"Merry Christmas, Michael." she said in her most alluring voice.

Michael was caught in a spell. The scent of her perfume filling his nostrils was sending him into a delirious rapture.

"Come in." he vaguely heard her say through the fog in his head.

As he stepped into the living room and removed his coat, his senses were slowly returning, but he resisted the return to full cognizance. He was enjoying the euphoric state he was in. All sorts of scattered thoughts were starting to sink in. All his planning for this evening had fallen apart. Jenny had issued a pre-emptive strike by kissing him before he could make his move. He was glad she did. Now the pressure was off. Through that one little kiss, he now knew how she felt. No more wondering, no more doubting needed. He could now just enjoy their evening together. Yet, the magical glow still lingered in the air, mixed in with Jenny's perfume.

Jenny went over and turned on the Christmas tree lights. The room was awash in a combination of candlelight and Christmas tree lights. Michael noticed the stacks of presents around the tree, as Jenny took his arm and ushered him towards the dining area. She had a fondue pot set out on the table, along with various cheeses, crackers, fruit slices, and Christmas cookies. She picked up a glass of white wine for herself and handed Michael another glass.

"Merry Christmas." she said once again, lifting her glass in a toast.

"Uh ..." Michael looked down at his glass.

"Relax. Yours is ginger ale."

He smiled and repeated "Merry Christmas" softly, as he took a sip of soda.

The low lights, his own tiredness, Jenny's dress, and Jenny herself were all combining to keep him disoriented in a splendid stupor. After taking some snacks onto a plate, they went to their familiar places at the couch, where they sat in silence, looking at the tree and each other.

Jenny finally broke the silence. "This is nice." she reflected, and after a pause, she continued. "Christmas can be a very lonely time. I'm glad you could come over."

"So am I." He wasn't in a talkative mood, preferring to just breathe and take everything in.

"I probably spent too much on the girls this year." she said, more to herself than to Michael, as she stared at the presents under the tree. "But I can't help myself at Christmas. I want them to have happy memories when they're older."

Jenny sat upright and moved closer to Michael. She looked deep into his eyes as she asked, "What was your favorite Christmas present ever?"

Michael smiled. "It's funny you should ask me that. I was just thinking about it the other day. One year I got this wood burning tool with a carving kit. It was what I had wanted for years, but my father always said I was too young. But then one year I got it. It's the only present I really remember, other than the year I got an electric razor."

He paused, reflected. "I guess both were symbols of adulthood." He sat up and edged towards Jenny. "But the best was the wood burning kit. It told me that my father thought I was okay. It's what got me started in my interest in wood carving."

"My best present" Jenny began, licking her lips like a little girl, "was when I was 14. It was just after my father died. It wasn't really a very happy Christmas, but my mother tried her best. She got me this cat, a beautiful white Persian. It looked like a big ball of cotton. I called her Snowball because she was so white and round. Snowball was my best friend for a while. She helped me get through the loss of my father."

"Funny." Michael came to a sudden realization. "Now that I think about it, I was 13 when I got that wood carving kit. It was after my mother died."

They were both quiet for a while.

"What happened to Snowball?" Michael asked innocently.

"Oh, she got crushed under a garage door."

"Oh." Michael hadn't expected such a morbid answer told in such a casual manner.

"Yeah, that was my last cat. We never got another one. I still miss her."

The evening moved along slowly. From time to time Michael gave some thought to leaving and getting on his way to Pennsylvania. But he was having too nice a time to leave. Several hours slowly ticked by, as the snow continued to fall outside. Once again, Jenny had fallen asleep on the couch. But this time she was sleeping peacefully, cradled in Michael's arms.

He knew he should leave and be on the road, but he was unwilling to let go of the moment. The feel of her head nestled on his chest filled him with a sort of well-being he couldn't describe. He thought about excuses he could make to his family for being late. Finally, he decided to just tell them he had another service to do Christmas morning. Why not? They didn't understand about why he had to go to church on Christmas Eve anyway. What was one more little thing to not understand?

His eyelids fought to stay open. He knew that he should at least get some sleep on the couch so that he would be able to drive in the morning. But again, he was unwilling to let sleep deprive him of taking in every moment of this wonderful feeling he was experiencing. He stayed awake.

◆◆◆

The brightness of the snow coming down made it difficult to determine what time of night it was. Michael's watch was buried under Jenny's hair. Daybreak snuck upon them.

Better than a clock was a child's sense of when Christmas had arrived. Becky shouted from her room, "Mommy, can we come out yet to see our presents?"

At the sound of her voice, Jenny jumped up from Michael's chest and wiped the sleep from her eyes. Quickly assessing the situation, she called back, "Just a minute, honey." She then got up and gathered herself together. Her dress was quite wrinkled. Her hair was going in all directions.

She looked at Michael, who had fear in his eyes. "Don't worry. She won't come out until I say it's all right. She knows Santa won't come if she comes out too early."

She lifted Michael off the couch by his arms and started ushering him out the door. "But you've got to get out of here."

"But, but ..." Things were happening way too fast for him.

"Shh. Quietly. Go outside for a few minutes and then ring the doorbell. I'll say that you just showed up to watch them open presents."

"But I need my coat."

She grabbed his coat and threw it towards him.

"Hurry." she said, as she closed the door behind him, barely avoiding catching the coat in the doorway.

He waited outside in the cold for a few minutes. It had stopped snowing, but everything was clothed in white, including his car. The street looked to have about four inches of snow covering it. It was not going to be an easy drive back home. He looked at his watch. It was after 6:30. There was no way he was going to make it back for the fun of watching Julia and Ryan opening their presents. But there were two other little children he could be watching. And it felt awfully cold outside. He rang the doorbell.

"Well, well, look who's here." Jenny said loudly, as Becky and Lisa gave a glance his way. They were more interested in the pile of presents under the tree.

"Look, girls. Michael's come to watch you open your presents."

"Why?" Becky asked, point-blank.

Jenny had no answer.

Michael stepped in. "Because I brought some more presents for you, and I wanted to make sure you got them for Christmas."

"Where are they?" Lisa asked.

"I left them in the car."

"Why didn't you bring them in with you?" Becky sounded like an interrogation officer.

Jenny stood motionless.

"I don't know." he said, feeling stupid. "Why don't I go back and get them."

"Can we open our presents now?" Becky pleaded.

"No, wait for Michael." she answered.

"Oh-h-h." Becky whined.

"I'll be right back." He went out to the car to get the presents that he had brought to give Jenny and the girls. He had left them in the trunk. It took a while to shove the snow off the trunk, but he went as fast as he could.

"Now can we open our presents?" Becky bellowed, as Michael stepped back inside the house.

"Why don't you open Michael's present first?" Jenny suggested.

"Oh-h-h."

Michael handed each of the girls a present. Becky tore into hers while Lisa carefully unwrapped her wrapping paper.

"What is it?" Jenny asked Becky, taking a seat on the couch.

"It's a watch." Becky said. "With Minnie Mouse on it!"

"O-o-o." Jenny cooed. "You like Minnie Mouse. What do you say?"

"Neat."

"Rebeccah."

"Thank you, Michael." Becky said, as she came over and gave him a hug.

"You're welcome." he said, a little embarrassed by the show of affection.

"What did you get, Lisa?" Jenny asked.

"Coloring books! And crayons!" she said excitedly, holding them up for her mother to see. "Thank you, Michael." she said, looking up quickly, before putting her head back down to begin coloring in one of the books.

"Can we open the other presents now?" Becky asked, more calmly now.

"Yes, go ahead."

Becky began tearing into the next box. Lisa continued to color. Michael took a seat next to Jenny.

"This one's for you." he said, handing her a small wrapped package.

She opened it carefully. Inside was a small jewelry box. She opened the lid slowly, while giving Michael a questioning glance.

"Oh, Michael." she said, gently lifting a gold chain from the box. "It's lovely." She studied the simple gold cross on the necklace. "I really like this."

"What is it, Mommy?" Becky asked, briefly losing interest in her own presents.

"Look." She held out the necklace for the girls to see. They didn't seem too impressed.

"We got you a present too." she said to Michael. "Becky, get the present at the back of the tree, the one we got for Michael."

"Oh yeah." Becky replied in recognition. She pulled out a small present, wrapped in different paper from the others. Then she walked over and handed it to Michael."

"What do you say?" Jenny said to Michael.

"Neat."

"Michael."

"Thank you, Becky." he replied.

He ripped the paper open. It was a book about The Beatles, one that he already had. But he appreciated the thought. He was just happy that Jenny had thought of him.

"Wow, this is great!" he said, thumbing through the pages of the book.

"Rebeccah picked it out." Jenny said, as Becky beamed. "You don't already have it, do you?"

"No, no." he answered, almost too emphatically. "It's one I wanted to get, but I never got around to buying it. I can't wait to start reading it. Thank you."

As he watched the girls open the last of their presents, guilt started overtaking him that he should be home opening presents with his own family. Hesitantly, he stood up to be on his way.

"Michael's leaving now." Jenny announced to the girls. "Say goodbye."

"Goodbye." they both quickly called over their shoulders, their attention focused on their favorite presents.

"Well, I really had a nice time last night and this morning." Michael said to Jenny. "I hate to leave. But I'll be back in two days. We can spend New Year's together."

"Uh, well, drive safely." Jenny's face looked pained.

"Well, thanks again." Michael leaned over to kiss Jenny goodbye. She turned her face away.

"Not in front of the girls." she said.

Michael looked over. Both girls had their backs turned to them. Once again, that old feeling of confusion that Michael got around Jenny returned.

"Well, I better get going." he said, resignation in his voice.

Jenny walked him to the door and watched as he cleared all the snow off his car. She waved as he pulled away.

Once he got off her street, after some difficulty, he found that the main roadways were plowed. His tiredness began to give him a tremendous fight. But he managed to stay awake by conjuring up images of Jenny lying in his arms. He had never taken off his scarf throughout the night, and the scent of her perfume had permeated the scarf's material and was now rising up into his nostrils, helping him to feel her presence. Despite the tiredness and the rotten driving conditions, it was a great drive back to Lancaster.

CHAPTER TEN

now

He put it off for as long as possible. No use upsetting the girls as long as there was a chance things would work out differently. But the time had come. They were coming tomorrow. Their first supervised visit. Michael needed to let Becky and Lisa know that a big change was coming into their lives. At his sister's suggestion, he decided to break the news to them at her house after having a family dinner together.

It was Julie who led them into the conversation.

"So girls," she started, as they all sat around the dinner table – she on one end, her husband Roger on the other end, their two children, Julia and Ryan on one side, Michael, Becky and Lisa crowded together on the other side. "Isn't it nice to be together as a family like this?"

Becky and Lisa ignored the question.

"I guess this takes a little getting used to." she plowed on, undeterred. "You know, having a new aunt and uncle and new cousins."

"We're not new, Mom." Ryan interjected. "We've always been here. They're the new ones."

"Quiet, Ryan. Your mother's talking." Roger's tone was enough to keep his son silent.

"Becky, it's nice having extended family, isn't it?" Julie suggested.

"I guess." Becky answered, concentrating more on her dinner.

"What's 's-tended' mean?" Lisa asked.

"Extended." Michael answered. "It means that you have more relatives than just me. You have Aunt Julie and Uncle Roger. And Julia and Ryan are your cousins. We're all one big family."

"And Mommy too." Lisa said simply.

"Yes, of course." Michael said softly. "Mommy will always be at the center of our family."

Michael saw this as his cue, and he gave Julie a silent nod.

"How about we have dessert in the living room?" she announced. "Julia, Ryan, help me clear the table and get dessert ready in the kitchen."

"But I'm still eating." Ryan objected.

"Ryan." Once again, Roger's tone was enough to get both siblings to comply. They all got up, grabbed their own plates, and headed off into the kitchen, leaving Michael alone with Becky and Lisa.

"While we're on the subject of family," Michael began nervously, "there's something I need to talk to you about."

"Uh oh." Becky rolled her eyes.

"No, this is a good thing." Michael began speeding up, before he lost his nerve. "You see, you not only have cousins, and an aunt and an uncle, but you have grandparents."

"Yes, we know." Becky said. "Grandma and Grandpa Griggs."

Michael was surprised by Becky's words. His father and step-mother were not involved in their lives at all.

"How do you know about them?" Michael asked.

"Julia and Ryan talk about them. That's their picture over there." Becky pointed to a framed photograph on the dining room hutch, showing his parents with Julia and Ryan when they were much younger.

"Well, you're right about that. But you know you have another set of grandparents too."

"Mommy's Mommy and Daddy?" Lisa asked.

"Well, no. They're no longer with us."

"Where are they?" Lisa asked.

"They're with Mommy in heaven." Becky explained to her younger sister.

"Oh."

"But you do have other grandparents." Michael continued.

"Who?" Becky asked.

"Grandma and Grandpa Farley. Your Daddy's parents."

"I didn't know that." Lisa gasped.

"How come we've never heard about them before?" Becky cut right to the heart of the matter.

"Well, I didn't know about them. And the thing is ... they didn't know about you until recently either."

"Huh?" Lisa was confused.

"Didn't our Daddy tell them about us?" Becky's quick grasp of the situation was far beyond her years.

"No, evidently he didn't."

"Why not?" Becky asked.

"I don't know the answer to that, honey. We've never talked about your Daddy before. What do you remember about him?"

"Nothing." Becky answered matter-of-factly. "We only know what Mommy told us, that he wasn't able to take care of us, so he had to leave."

"Nothing else?"

Becky thought for a moment before answering.

"No, not really. We never really talked about him. Or thought about him. Did you talk to him?"

"No, honey. I just found out that he's gone now too."

"Gone where?" Lisa asked.

"To heaven." Becky replied.

"Oh."

"But I did talk to his parents. Your grandparents. Their names are Gerald and Mildred, and they're really anxious to meet you." Michael paused and took in a deep breath. "In fact, they're coming by tomorrow to see you." He stopped to gauge their reaction. But their faces were unchanged. "So, what do you think about that?"

"Neat." Lisa said simply.

"Becky?"

"Okay, I guess. Can we get dessert now?"

There was more Michael needed to say. He needed to tell them about the woman who would be with them on their visit. Why she was there and why she might be asking them certain questions. Why there would be more visits with the Farley's. Why things would be changing. But all this could wait until the morning. The girls were ready to move onto other things. He was too.

"Yeah, let's get dessert. I hope it's ice cream."

"I hope it's pink!" Lisa chirped.

"You always hope it's pink." Becky countered.

It was another agonizing, sleepless night waiting for morning to come. The night seemed to be lasting forever, yet the morning seemed to come way too soon. He dragged himself out of bed, took a shower to clear his head, and then went down to make breakfast. Before he had a chance to go back upstairs to wake the girls, they appeared together in the kitchen.

"Good morning girls. Breakfast is ready. Come sit and eat."

Becky and Lisa sat at the kitchen table and helped themselves to the stack of pancakes in front of them. Michael joined them at the table and poured a glass of orange juice for himself.

"You know what's happening today, right?" he asked, receiving only nods in response. "Your grandparents are coming. They'll be here in about two hours."

"What are we going to be doing with them?" Becky asked, while stuffing a way too big portion of a pancake into her mouth.

"I'm not sure, but I'm sure they'll be taking you somewhere nice."

"Are you going too?" Becky asked.

"No. I'll stay here and I'll be here when you get back. But there will be another lady going with you."

"Who?"

"Well, I don't remember her name. Anita something. I've only talked to her on the phone. She'll be coming just to help you get to know your grandparents better. She's like a ... Well, like a Teacher's Aide, like Miss Lucy from your class. She'll be there to help in case you or your grandparents need anything."

"I forgot their names." Lisa said.

"You mean your grandparents? Your Grandma's first name is Mildred and your Grandpa's name is Gerald."

"What should we call them?" Becky asked.

"Probably just Grandma and Grandpa will be fine. But you can ask them when they get here."

"Do we have to go?" Becky asked.

"Well, yes you do. But try not to look at it like a bad thing. You'll have fun. They're your grandparents. They're a part of your family. Do you have any other questions?"

They both nodded no.

"Then finish eating so you can get dressed and be ready to go when they get here."

••••◆◆◆••••

The girls sat with their knees against the back of the couch looking out the window.

"There's a car stopping." Becky announced. "People are getting out. They look old. It must be them."

Michael joined the girls at the window. He studied the three people coming up the walkway. The social worker was easy to pick out. She was wearing a dark business suit, with her hair tied neatly back. She didn't look any older than him. The other two surprised him. He was expecting a frail, elderly couple. At least that was what he was hoping for. A couple too old to keep up with two small children would go a long way in his favor in a court decision. But these two getting ever closer to his door looked more like they were in their 50's. The man was short, thin, fit looking. His hair was thinning and mostly gray, but his face was free of any age lines. He was wearing a hooded sweatshirt, jeans, and sneakers. His wife was also short, not quite as thin, but not overweight either. Her blonde hair was cut short, very stylishly. She too was dressed casually, but Michael could tell she put more time into putting her outfit together. Overall, they both looked quite capable of caring for two children. Michael became more worried.

At the sound of the doorbell, Michael moved toward the door, with the girls following close behind.

"Mr. Griggs? I'm Anita Bamert. I've been assigned to this case." The young woman handed Michael her card as she made her way inside.

"Yes, I know." Michael said, stepping aside for the woman pushing past him. "We spoke on the phone."

"These are the Farley's – Mildred and Gerald." she said, turning toward the couple still standing outside.

Michael started to greet them, but was stopped by the gasp that came out of Mildred Farley's mouth. It was clear from her face that she was overwhelmed by the sight of the two girls standing in front of her, as she clutched her hands to her chest.

"Oh my." she said, stepping gingerly inside the house. "They look just like John."

She started to reach out to touch them, but stopped herself. Looking toward the social worker, she asked, "Is it all right …?"

Anita nodded.

Mildred extended her hand toward Becky.

"You must be Rebeccah. I'm … well, I'm Mildred. I'm your Daddy's Mommy."

"Hello." Becky shook Mildred's hand.

"And you must be Lisa." Mildred took in another deep breath, shaking Lisa's hand.

"Can we call you Grandma?" Lisa asked.

"You certainly may." Mildred's face looked like it was holding back tears.

"And you can call me Grandpa." Gerald made his way forward to join his wife, as he shook both girls' hands.

"Why don't we go into the living room?" Michael suggested.

"Oh, I'm sorry." Mildred, for the first time since laying her eyes on the girls, looked up at Michael. "We didn't introduce ourselves. I'm Mildred. And this is my husband, Gerald."

Gerald extended his hand to Michael, and the two men shook hands. The two then exchanged hellos.

No one made any effort to move closer into the living room. Instead, they all stood in place.

"Mr. Griggs …" Mildred began, breaking the awkward silence.

"Call me Mike, er, Michael." Michael wanted to hate these people, but he was finding it very hard to dislike them.

"Thank you, Michael. I just wanted to let you know that we're sorry for any distress this may have caused you. We really don't want to cause you any trouble. We just really needed to meet these two lovely children. We want to …, well we …, it's just that our son John was all we had. Now that he's gone …" She seemed to be drifting off. "We made so many mistakes with him. We …"

"Perhaps it would be better that we not say too much right now, Mildred." Gerald took hold of his wife's waist. "Maybe we should be getting started with the day we have planned."

"That's probably a good idea." Anita affirmed. "We can talk tonight when we drop the girls back here. We'll be back no later than 8:00."

"Yes, yes." Mildred agreed. "Girls, we're going to have such fun together. We can't wait."

Becky and Lisa looked to Michael.

"It's all right." he said quietly. "Go ahead. Have fun. But bring your coats. It's going to get cold tonight."

The girls got their coats from the coat rack and started out the door, being escorted by Anita and the Farley's. They took one last look back before the door closed.

"I'll be right here." Michael assured them. "I'm not going anywhere."

With that the door closed and Michael felt something slam shut inside him – his world.

CHAPTER ELEVEN

then

Instead of going with his original story of having a Christmas morning worship service to do, Michael used the snow storm as an excuse to his family for his getting such a late start. Neither his father nor his stepmother were religious people, and they did not understand the concept of worship as work. His sister, who had always been a churchgoer, would have bought it. However, she did not buy the snow excuse.

"Since when has snow ever stopped you before?" she said to him privately after he had settled in. "Tell the truth, Mike. Who's the girl?"

He could never hide anything from Julie. He could always confide in his older sister. While sitting alone together in the kitchen, he told her all about Jenny.

"Just don't tell Dad." was her only advice to him. "He'd flip if he heard you were dating a divorced woman."

He enjoyed the visit with the family. He had been away for too long. Though he always felt uncomfortable being around his father and stepmother for any length of time, he was getting closer to his sister as they both moved into adulthood. Her husband, Roger, was a nice enough guy. At least he was easy to talk to. And it was great to see Ryan and Julia. He was amazed at how much they had grown since he last saw them. He had missed both their last birthdays. Julia was now twelve, and Ryan had just turned ten. Every time he watched them playing with their toys around the Christmas tree, he was reminded of Lisa and Becky. Everything he did around the house reminded him of Jenny.

He was tempted to call her, but there were no ideal moments away from the rest of the family to sneak a call in. Finally, the urge overwhelmed him and he made a quick call from the bathroom. A man answered. Michael quickly hung up without saying anything. He must have misdialed, he thought. He was never very good with phones. At any rate, he had gotten the urge out of his system. He decided to wait until he got back to Holmdel to call again.

He slept well Christmas night, back in his old room and old bed. Julie and Roger left with the kids after breakfast the next morning. Michael had planned to stay until that evening, but he was growing too restless in the house alone with his parents. He would rather be back with Jenny. Finally, by mid-afternoon he had resolved to go back. He now used the excuse that he had some work to attend to. His parents may not have understood religion, but they both understood the work ethic. They did not put up an argument at his leaving.

❖❖❖

He arrived back at his apartment before nine p.m. After taking care of a few necessary things, he called Jenny.

"I thought you wouldn't be back until tomorrow." she said, surprised.

"I decided to leave early." he replied enthusiastically. "I missed you."

Jenny made no response.

Michael was hoping for an invitation to come over. Since no offer was forthcoming, he moved on to his next proposition.

"So anyway, how about New Year's Eve? Was there anything special you wanted to do? It's going to be kind of hard making a reservation at this late date."

There was a pause on the other end of the line.

"Michael, I ..." Jenny started to say something, but did not finish her thought.

"What? What's wrong?" he asked.

"Nothing. Look, let's talk tomorrow, all right?"

"Jenny, you don't sound right. What's the matter?"

"Nothing." There was clear agitation in her voice. "Let's just talk tomorrow. Please."

"Okay." he answered hesitantly. "I'll call you tomorrow. Goodnight."

"Goodnight, Michael." she said, closing the conversation. But then, she quickly added "Oh, and Michael? I'm glad you're back."

She hung up.

At least there was that, he thought to himself. She was glad he was back. But he sure was confused all over again.

It was a restless night. Michael could never sleep when something was weighing on his mind. And the phone conversation was definitely weighing on his mind.

He went to work the next morning, but he couldn't stay in his office for very long. He was too worked up. He left before noon to drive over to Jenny's.

"Michael!" Jenny said, surprised to see him at the door. "What are you doing here?"

"You just sounded upset or something on the phone last night. I wanted to see what it was all about. Can I come in?"

"Yes, all right. Come in. We might as well get this over with."

She stepped aside and he entered the living room.

"Get what over with?" he asked, standing in the center of the room. "Jenny, what's going on? I'm all confused."

"I know. I'm sorry. I knew this would happen."

"You're scaring me. Will you please tell me what's wrong?"

Jenny's arms kept going up to and down from her face to her hips. "Michael, have a seat."

He took a seat on the couch and she sat beside him.

"It's about New Year's Eve." she said, after taking a deep breath.

"Yeah? What about it?"

"I was going to lie and make up some excuse. But I can't do that to you. The truth is, I have another date for New Year's."

Michael sat back further into the couch.

"I don't understand." he said blankly. "What about Christmas? I thought it was special for you like it was for me."

"It was." she said firmly, taking his hand in hers. "I made this date before Christmas, over a month ago."

"Then just break it."

"I can't."

"Why not?"

"It wouldn't be right."

Michael pulled his hand away.

"And this is?"

"Michael, he's an old friend. We get together every New Year's Eve to keep each other company. There's nothing more to it. I can't just cancel it at this late date and leave him stranded. Please understand."

"I understand what you're saying." he said calmly. "But I don't understand your logic. You'd rather hurt me than him?"

"You see!" she said, jumping on his comment. "I told you you'd get hurt. I tried to warn you. Now you're hurt, and it's hurting me too. I hate this."

"Just tell me one thing honestly." He structured his next thoughts carefully. "Christmas night, I called here. A man answered your phone. Was that him?"

She looked into his eyes.

"Yes." she said simply.

Michael sprang up from the couch and started for the door. Tears were beginning to form in his eyes.

"I have to leave." was all he could manage to say.

Jenny called to him.

"Michael, don't leave like this."

She grabbed his arm to stop him.

"You don't understand how lonely it gets for me around the holidays. My whole life is Rebeccah and Lisa. But I need adult companionship sometimes too. He's just a friend. How can I make you understand that?"

"I'm sorry." he said, breaking free. "I just can't deal with this right now. I have to go."

He rushed out the door and sped away in his car, wiping the tears off his cheeks.

••• ◈ ◈ ◈ •••

Once again, he buried himself in his work, spending the rest of the day locked in his office, planning for a winter Youth Group retreat. He filled his next day's calendar making hospital and shut-in visits. All the while, Jenny was foremost on his mind.

After getting over his own hurt, he began to try to see things from her perspective. He found that he could understand her position. He had taken for granted how difficult it must have been for her to raise two children on her own. He could only guess how lonely it must get at times. Though it would hurt that she was spending New Year's Eve with someone else, he held no monopoly on her time. He shouldn't have presumed that she would be free. He could deal with the hurt as long as he was somewhere in the running for Jenny's attention. He resolved to call her later when he got home and apologize.

As Michael walked in the door of his apartment that evening, the phone was ringing. It was Jenny.

"Michael?" Her voice on the other end of the line made Michael feel better. "Where have you been? I stopped at the church earlier looking for you. And I've been calling for hours."

"Yeah, I had a lot of visits to make today. I've been on the road all day."

"Are you still mad?"

"No. I'm okay." Michael plopped himself down on his couch.

"Listen, I called my friend and canceled our date for New Year's. So I'm available if you're still free."

Michael almost jumped off the couch.

"Sure. Great. But I'm positive we won't be able to get a reservation anywhere now."

"There's an opening at my place," she suggested, "if you don't mind spending New Year's Eve with two rambunctious children."

"No, that sounds like fun. If you want, I'll bring over some board games that we all can play."

"Fine. I'll provide the refreshments. It'll be a wild celebration."

"As long as we're together." Michael said seriously. "And look, I'm glad you did it, but I hope you don't feel bad about canceling your other date."

"No. I explained it to him and he understood. And Michael, just for the record, Christmas night …"

"Yeah?" he said nervously.

"All I did was talk about you the whole time. And he talked about a woman he was seeing. He left early, and I spent the rest of the night missing you. Okay?"

"Okay. Thanks. I'll talk to you tomorrow."

It looked like calm seas were finally on the horizon.

❖❖❖

Michael remembered when he was very young and would stay up on New Year's Eve playing games with his mother and father and sister. It was one of the few memories he had of family togetherness. It was another tradition that died with the death of his mother. He was happy for the opportunity to renew the tradition with Jenny's family. He preferred it to a noisy celebration in some public venue.

He looked at the few board games he had brought with him from home. None of them were suitable for children under the age of eight. On New Year's Eve day he went to a toy store to buy some games they all could play. Looking over the shelves of board games stacked up was like taking a trip back in time. Different games brought back memories of birthdays and Christmases from various stages of his childhood. He picked several of his favorites, including his all-time favorite, Candy Land. It was his very first game. He could play it for hours and never grow tired of it.

He arrived at the house at dinnertime. Jenny was dressed up in a simple, yet alluring black gown, with a sparkling gold jacket over it. He felt slightly underdressed in his jeans and old sweater. They enjoyed a simple chicken dinner together before turning on the television and setting up the first board game. Michael picked Candy Land. Jenny set out snacks while the girls got the game ready. It was the perfect kind of evening for Michael - his favorite dinner, playing games, watching TV, plenty of munchies. Jenny even had bottles of soda out.

"A special treat for New Year's." she said. "The caffeine will help the girls stay awake for midnight."

They played the first game several times. Lisa loved playing Candy Land. Becky was ready to move on to something else. So was Michael. It wasn't as exciting as he had remembered it from when he was four years old. They played a few more times before moving on to something else. Jenny would play the first round of each new game they brought out, then excuse herself to take care of the snacks. Michael hung in for every game. They played for four hours.

"It's getting close to midnight, girls." Jenny announced, as they finished another game. "Why don't you put the games away and watch the ball drop on television."

They left the games scattered about the floor and took their usual seats. Lisa sat on the rocker and Becky sat on the black chair. Michael and Jenny took their places on the couch, as Jenny explained to the girls how a ball dropped to welcome in the new year. Michael didn't pay much attention to the television broadcast. He was thinking about the traditional New Year's kiss and how he should make his move. The new year was about fifteen minutes away.

He thought about the significance of a new year, and wondered about what this new year would bring. Where would it lead Jenny and him? Everything felt right and natural. Would it last? He was determined to make it work. The new year would be a brand new start, and he was ready to start it out on a positive note with a passionate kiss.

The minute countdown began on the television. He looked around the room. The girls were sound asleep. Good. He wouldn't need to feel embarrassed kissing their mother in front of them. Unfortunately, as he turned his head, he discovered that Jenny was also sleeping soundly. The countdown passed. It was a new year. He welcomed it alone.

CHAPTER TWELVE

now

It was a long day for him. He spent the first part of it cleaning up around the house. But there wasn't that much to clean. He had already gone through the entire house cleaning up everything he could find in anticipation of the social worker's first visit. He wanted to be prepared for any inspection tour. He was frankly surprised that there wasn't an inspection. Maybe that would take place when they got back. So he made doubly sure everything was sparkling clean.

He tried to find other things to keep him busy. He thought about going for a walk, but was afraid to leave the house in case they came back early. He went out to the garage and tried to lose himself in some woodwork. But he couldn't concentrate. He tried several different times to eat, but had no appetite. So he did the only thing that took him out of his own head – watched TV. There was nothing good on, but he sat and watched anyway.

As the sky turned dark, he got up several times to look out the window. Whenever he heard a car, he got up to check. Eight o'clock came, but still no sign of them. Now his anxiety turned to worry. But at 8:11 the car pulled up. He watched the girls get out of the car, then ran back and turned off the TV before going to the door to open it before anyone even reached it.

Becky and Lisa ran in, right past Michael. The three adults followed shortly after.

"Sorry we're late." Anita said apologetically. "It was my fault. I was having such a good time, I lost track of the time."

"Well, just as long as you were having fun." Michael said dryly.

He turned his attention to the girls, who were giggling and dancing around. He recognized that look. They were hopped up on sugar.

"Did you have a good time, girls?" he asked.

"It was awesome!" Becky exclaimed.

"Grandma and Grandpa are the best!" Lisa proclaimed.

Michael's heart was sinking. It's not that he didn't want them having a good time. He just wasn't expecting them to be so happy. And calling them Grandma and Grandpa? Really? Already?

Before he was cognizant of it, the adults had removed their jackets and made themselves comfortable in seats in the living room, as the girls continued to dance about in the middle of the room. It was as if they had already taken over and he was already half way out the door of his own house. But no, it wasn't really his house. It was Jenny's, which meant the house was more Becky's and Lisa's than his. Could they possibly take that away from him too? He tried to push the thought out of his head and keep himself in the game.

"So what did you all do today?" he asked to no one in particular as he sat on a foot rest, as all the seats had been taken.

"We went to the zoo!" Lisa exclaimed.

"The petting zoo over in Holmdel Park." Mildred volunteered.

"Yeah!" Lisa continued. "And we got to feed all sorts of animals."

"That's great." Michael said, with no enthusiasm. "What else did you do?"

"We got ice cream and went to a toy store and a candy store and … uh, I forget." Lisa said.

"We got our costumes." Becky added.

"Oh yeah. We got our costumes." Lisa said.

"What? What costumes?" Michael asked.

"Our Halloween costumes for next week." Becky responded. "I'm going as a Butterfly Princess."

"And I'm a Bumble Bee!" Lisa chimed in.

"We hope you don't mind, Michael." Mildred spoke up. "They said they hadn't gotten their costumes yet. And Halloween is next week. We thought maybe you didn't have the time for shopping."

"What? No, I have the time. I just forgot. I mean, with everything going on, it just slipped my mind."

"Are you sure it's all right?" Mildred asked.

"What? Yeah, sure. No, I mean, uh, no, that's fine." Michael was upset, but he wasn't sure if he was more upset by their presumption or by his own negligence. He was trying to keep his cool and not lose it in front of the social worker.

"While we're on the subject," Mildred began tentatively, "we were hoping that as Halloween is next week that we might take the girls Trick or Treating for our next visit. We asked the girls and they're fine with it. We also talked it over with Anita and she's okay with it."

"Well, just as long as Anita approves." His dripping sarcasm came out louder than he intended.

"What?" Fortunately, Anita only heard her name mentioned, nothing more.

"Nothing." Michael said. "Let me think about it."

"Can Grandma and Grandpa take us, please?" Becky pleaded.

"It would be a good bonding opportunity for me to observe." Anita suggested.

"Fine. Whatever. Okay, sure. You can take them."

"Yay!" Lisa proclaimed.

Michael felt his world getting ever smaller, as he felt it getting harder and harder to breathe.

CHAPTER THIRTEEN

then

I t was a cold January morning. He was enjoying his day off hanging around the apartment. Then she called.

"Do you want to go sledding?" Jenny asked simply.

"Sure, that sounds like fun." Michael responded. "The girls should enjoy that."

"Nuh-uh." Jenny corrected. "No little folk this time. Just you and me."

"Are you serious?"

"Totally. The girls are spending the day with my neighbor next door and her kids. So, do you still want to come out and play?"

"You bet I do. I'm on my way over."

They drove to Holmdel Park. Then they got out and began walking, taking turns dragging the sled behind them.

"How far are we going?" Michael asked.

"You'll see. I know this private place where there's a big hill we can go down."

They kept walking. It was a twenty minute walk through the huge park before they got to the site Jenny had picked out.

"That is a big hill." Michael said, looking up. "And long. We're going to be here all day going up and down this thing."

"I've got nothing else to do today." she smiled. "You?"

"Let's do it."

They reached the top of the hill and, despite the cold, Michael found himself sweating. They stood for a moment, catching their breath and gazing down at the hill, which seemed even higher and longer from this viewpoint.

Jenny gave Michael a nudge. "You go first."

"Boy, I haven't done this since college." he said, as he began placing the sled into proper position.

"I haven't done it since I was a little girl. Now go on. Show me how it's done."

"Okay, here goes nothing."

Lying on top of the sled, he pushed off. But the sled's runners sank into the snow. He slid forward, while the sled remained firmly in place.

"That was nothing, all right." she laughed.

"Hang on a minute." he said, picking himself up, then lifting the runners out of the snow. "It's coming back to me now. I just need to make a running start with this thing."

He picked up the sled and backed up from the edge of the hill. Then he charged forward, slammed the sled to the ground, and jumped on top. He immediately fell off, as the sled continued on down the hill on its own. Jenny burst out laughing.

"Well, go get it, Slim." she teased, pointing to the sled at the bottom of the hill.

"I'm glad you're enjoying this." he grumbled, as he started down the hill.

"I am. I really am." She smiled broadly.

He got it right on his third attempt. It was a great ride down the hill. He felt the rush of excitement coming back from younger days. At the end of the ride, he started laughing.

"All right! Nice ride." Jenny cheered, as he made his way back up to the top of the hill.

"Okay, now it's your turn to show what you can do."

She put the sled down at the edge of the hill, got on top, and tried to push off. The sled didn't move.

"You've got to get a running start." he advised.

"But I can't do it that way. I'm afraid."

"Oh don't be a baby. Come on, try it."

She picked up the sled, stepped back, and then ran forward. She let go of the sled, but didn't jump on.

"Slick move, Clyde." he said, as the sled proceeded on down the hill without a rider. "Now you get to go down the hill and get it."

"Can't you get it for me?" she said in a little girl's voice.

"No. I got it last time. It's your turn."

"Ple-e-e-ase." she begged in a drawn out baby's voice, grabbing his coat collar in her fists. "You're a man and I'm just a girl. Retrieving sleds is your job."

"Whatever happened to equal rights?"

"We never got them." she said. "Oh, please. I'll be your best friend."

She gave him a quick kiss on the lips.

"Well, when you put it that way."

He trekked down the hill and retrieved the sled.

"Okay." he announced once he had climbed back up. "This time you've got to jump onto the sled."

"That's easy for you to say. You don't have breasts to worry about." Then inspiration struck her. "I know! You jump on and get it started. Then I'll jump on top of you and we can both go down together."

Michael figured it would never work, but he was intrigued by the notion of trying. Jenny stood just below the edge of the hill as Michael made his run. To his surprise, she managed to climb on top of him, and they made it two-thirds of the way down the hill, before Jenny toppled off, taking Michael with her. They tumbled over each other a few times before coming to a stop, still clutching on to one another. They lay there laughing, neither of them wanting to move.

"I can't remember having this much fun in a long time." Jenny finally revealed. "I feel so young and alive again. Carefree. I think you're good for me, Michael."

"I'm glad."

"I mean it. For so many years, raising the girls alone, something was missing. It was like part of my life was eroding away."

She cleared some snow from his face.

"I wouldn't give up one moment of my time with the girls for anything." she continued. "But for the first time in a long time, I'm feeling like me again. You brought back the smile."

She gave him another quick kiss, cocked her head, and smiled, as she said, "And you know what? I think I might just love you."

"Oh yeah?" Michael's reaction was filled with joy. "Well, I know I do. Love you, that is."

"Good."

This time, Michael kissed her.

CHAPTER FOURTEEN

now

He sat in the lone chair in the middle of the long wooden table facing the six people seated together at the other side of the table. It reminded him of a laid-back firing squad. Sitting there in the Synod Office's conference room brought back memories of the other times he sat in the same chair at the same table facing the same members of the Candidacy Committee. Those other occasions had seemed so important back then and he had been extremely nervous each time. But their importance was miniscule compared to this meeting. And yet, he didn't feel anywhere near as nervous as he had back then. He was strangely calm. Calm and agitated at the same time. He wanted to get this over with. So far the questions had been mostly theologically based – softballs, he thought. But he knew what was coming. The personal questions. Why did you quit just when you were at the finishing line? Have you lost your faith? Why are you back here now?

He had thought about those questions and how he might answer them many times in his head. He still had no good answer to offer. He briefly entertained the thought of just lying, but this was no way to move forward. He resolved to answer as truthfully as he could, no matter the outcome. As to just what he would say, he wouldn't know himself until the words started coming out of his mouth.

Reverend Patricia Sloan, the chairwoman of the committee, who was seated directly opposite him, began the line of questioning that moved away from the theological to the personal.

"Mr. Griggs, I know that these past months have been a difficult time for you. Losing your wife must have been very hard on you. Could you tell the Committee a little about that journey you've been taking?"

"Journey?" he thought to himself. "You call this utter torture I've been through a journey? A journey is a train ride through the countryside. These last months have hardly been a journey. Are you looking for me to spill my guts in front of you? Good luck with that."

He took a moment to compose himself. If he had shared his real thoughts out loud, that would be the end of his chances. He tried to find a way to express his thoughts in a more presentable way.

"Well," he began, after taking a sip of water, "these months have been very difficult. But there's been so much that's gone through my head that I don't think I could adequately explain it to you. Losing someone like Jenny is not something you just get over. I still think about her almost every moment of every day. And truthfully, I haven't completely come to terms with why she was taken away from me. There have been a lot of sleepless nights, believe me. But I've had to move forward. I have two children to live for. And right now they are my reason for living."

"What do you mean by that?" one of the other clergy asked.

"They take me out of my thoughts. I can't let my grief consume me when I have to deal with making school lunches and helping with homework and cleaning scraped knees and dealing with tears from ..."

"From? Please continue."

Michael wasn't sure he wanted to continue, but he screwed up his courage. "These girls still miss their mother ... terribly. They still cry sometimes at night. Someone has to be there for them. And it turns out I'm that someone. I have to be strong for them."

Michael fought back tears forming along his lower eyelids.

"Perhaps we should take a five minute break." Pastor Sloan suggested.

"It's getting awfully late, Patricia." Reverend Steele protested from the far end of the table. "Let's keep this moving along so we can end at a reasonable time. I have a Reformation service at my church tonight I need to get ready for, and frankly I don't think Mr. Griggs has been very forthcoming in his responses. Maybe, sir, you can start being a little more cooperative with this committee."

"Reformation?!" Michael blurted out the word in anger, involuntarily. He knew he should stop himself, but he couldn't help exploding. "You're talking about a Reformation service? Well I have two little girls at home waiting for me to get back so that they can go out Trick or Treating. And, I can't believe I almost forgot this, today … today would be their mother's 28th birthday. I'm sure they didn't forget. They need to be out there getting candy and having fun and … and not dwelling on the sadness. And frankly, I care more about that right now than I do about answering any more of your questions."

After his sudden outburst, he wilted in his chair. He had blown it. There was no way they would approve him now.

"Well, I'll tell you …" Pastor Steele began, before being cut off by Melanie Swan, the sole layperson on the committee, who was sitting on the opposite end of Pastor Steele, and had been mostly silent up to this point.

"If I may say something, Madame Chairwoman." she began. "I think it's admirable that Mr. Griggs is putting the welfare of his daughters first. And I think he's right. It's Halloween. We should be home with our families."

"You make a good point, Mrs. Swan." Pastor Sloan responded. "I for one would like to see my grandchildren in their costumes. So

I suggest we adjourn for now and schedule another date in the near future to continue our discussion. All in favor?"

"Aye." came the unanimous vote and the meeting was adjourned.

Michael walked out with mixed feelings. While he wasn't looking forward to dragging out the process, at least the subject of his unbelief never came up. He would have some additional time to sort through all that. But for now, he had to get back home to see the girls in their costumes before they went out into the night with their grandparents – without him.

CHAPTER FIFTEEN

then

"I'm afraid I have to cancel dinner tonight." Jenny said, after dropping in on Michael at the church. "They called me in to work."

"That's all right." Michael said, understanding. "We can skip dinner together for one night. Can you stick around here for a while?"

"No, I'm afraid not. I've got to go and try to find a babysitter. All my regulars are busy tonight. I don't know what I'm going to do."

Michael pondered the situation for a moment, then made a bold proposal.

"Why don't I come over and stay with them?"

Jenny shot him a quizzical look.

"I don't think that's such a great idea."

"Why not? It would be a good opportunity to get to know them better. I've never spent any time alone with them before."

"That's why I don't think it'd be such a good idea."

Michael got up from his desk and put his hands on Jenny's shoulders.

"What other choice do you have? Look, I'll come over for dinner like we planned, and then I'll just stay with the girls until you get back. It'll be fine."

"Are you sure?" Jenny's face look unconvinced.

"Yes. Trust me. It'll be fine. It'll be fun."

"I'm beginning to question your concept of fun." Jenny's face relaxed a bit. "But all right. I don't think you know what you're getting yourself into, but you're right – I don't have any other choices."

She leaned back to pick up her purse from the chair, then gave him a quick kiss before heading towards the door.

"It was sweet of you to offer." she said, looking back. "I'll see you later."

Michael and the girls ate dinner while Jenny got dressed for work.

"You girls behave, and do what Michael tells you." she said, rushing into the room on her way out the door. "Goodbye, Michael. Good luck."

"We'll be fine." Michael smiled from the dinner table, as the seeds of doubt suddenly began to take root.

As soon as Jenny was out the door, the girls began running around and shouting like they were possessed. He had never seen them like this. He didn't understand what kind of change had come over them.

"Let's play a game, Michael." Becky said, as Lisa began pulling on his arm.

"Fine." he consented, figuring a game might calm them down. "Get one out and set it up while I finish my dinner."

Before he could finish his chicken, they were back from their bedrooms, each carrying an armful of games. Before long, the living room was littered with pieces from various board games. In between games, the girls made trips to the kitchen to load up on junk food.

"I think maybe you've eaten enough for tonight." he finally declared.

"Mom lets us eat as much as we want." Becky answered, gobbling down a handful of M&M's.

"I find that hard to believe." he responded. But it had no effect on the girls. They continued to ignore him. It was sinking in that he was in over his head.

The time Michael was dreading most arrived.

"It's bedtime girls. Go to bed now."

He knew from when he was a child that they would fight to stay up for as long as possible. So he wasn't surprised when they ignored him.

"Girls, I said it's time for bed." he stated in the most authoritative voice he could muster. "Your mother wanted you in bed by 9:00." He hoped that invoking their mother's name might carry some weight. He should have known better.

"Look, I'll make you a deal." he said, changing tactics. At least, this time he had gained their attention. "I'll let you stay up for an extra half hour if you go and put on your pajamas now."

"We don't have to do what you say." Becky answered, point-blank.

He knew he was being challenged. The only way to survive was by being firm.

"Okay, that's it! I want you both to get ready for bed right now!"

Lisa started up the stairs to her room. But Becky lingered. Michael took her by the arm and led her towards the stairway.

"Ow-w, you're hurting me!" she protested.

"Well, if you won't listen, then I'll have to put you to bed myself. Now what's it going to be?" He let go of her arm.

"I hate you. I hate you." Becky screamed as she ran up the stairs.

"Just wonderful." Michael said to himself. He really hated playing the role of authoritarian.

A few minutes later he walked up the stairs. He had only been upstairs briefly once before. There was a bathroom at the top of the stairs, and a narrow hallway leading to three bedrooms. The closest bedroom on the right was Lisa's. Michael looked in. She was climbing into bed. The far bedroom on the right belonged to Becky. The light was on, but she was in the bathroom. Michael took a quick peek into the bedroom on the left where Jenny slept. It was too dark to see much. He knocked on the bathroom door.

"What are you doing in there, Becky?" Immediately, he recognized the words as belonging to his father, not him.

"I'm brushing my teeth."

"Well hurry up. It's way past your bedtime."

He waited by the door. Instead of hearing the sounds of someone brushing their teeth, Michael heard Becky singing. He opened the partially closed door all the way and stepped inside. She was sitting on the edge of the bathtub. She looked startled at seeing him enter.

"Becky, you're really trying my patience. Let's go."

"I haven't brushed my teeth yet."

"Then do it."

"Are you gonna watch?"

"I sure am. I'll even brush your teeth for you if you don't get a move on."

Michael heard her grumble some words too softly to make out. Just as well, he thought. He wasn't in the mood for any more confrontation.

"All right." he said when she finished. "Now go straight to bed."

"I hope my Mommy never invites you over for dinner again." she said, her eyes trying to penetrate his.

It stung him deeply. He had thought the evening would be a good way to get closer to the girls. But it was having just the opposite effect.

He looked in to make sure that Becky was in bed. To his relief, she was.

"Do you want the light off?" he asked.

"I don't care." she answered, keeping her back to him.

He switched off the light. Then he checked in on Lisa. She was in bed, sitting up.

"Go to sleep, Lisa." he said.

"I'm not tired. Mommy always reads me a story before I go to bed."

He stepped into the room. His thoughts flashed back to early childhood memories.

"You know, when I was little, my mother used to tell me stories. Only she didn't get them from books. She made them up herself."

"What was your Mommy's name?" she asked.

"Julia."

"Make up a story for me."

Michael felt a surge of panic. He didn't know anything about making up stories. But he found himself talking, making things up as he went along.

"Once upon a time, there was a little girl who lived in a forest. It was a magical forest where all the trees and animals talked. But they only talked to the little girl. Her name was Doris."

"Doris?" she giggled.

"Yeah, Doris. Anyway, whenever anyone would come into the forest to visit, Doris would tell them about the talking trees and the animals that talked to her. She'd see a rabbit go by and say, 'Hey Mr. Bunny, talk to my new friend.' But the rabbit wouldn't say anything. Then she'd walk up to a tree and ask it to say hello. But the tree would keep quiet. The visitor would then leave the forest thinking that Doris was crazy. This made Doris mad."

"I'd be mad too. Those trees and rabbits weren't very nice."

"Doris would ask the bunny, 'Why didn't you say anything?' She'd ask the tree the same question. But all the animals and all the trees kept giving her the same answer. 'We only want to talk to you, Doris. You're our friend. We don't want to lose you. You might leave the forest with your new friends and forget about us.'

'That's silly.' Doris would answer. 'You can never have too many friends. Just because I'm friends with someone else doesn't mean I don't like you anymore. We'll always be friends. And you can make new friends if you just talk to them.'

'We can?' they asked. 'We didn't know that.' Well, from that day on, whenever someone new came into the forest, the trees and all the animals would say hello. And Doris and everyone in the forest kept making more and more friends until the day came when everyone was living in the forest. The whole world became one big forest where everyone was nice to everyone else. And everyone lived happily ever after. The end."

"That was good." Lisa said, sleep taking over. "Tell me another one."

"No, that's it for tonight. You need your sleep. Goodnight."

He began heading towards the door.

"Michael?"

"Yes?"

"Will you tell me another story tomorrow night?"

"We'll see. Goodnight now."

"G'night."

He turned off her light and went back downstairs.

He fell asleep on the couch, but woke up when Jenny came in the door a little past midnight.

"Hi." she said softly. She slipped next to him on the couch and snuggled close. "How'd it go?"

"Well, it was an experience. I'll say that anyway."

"Did they give you a hard time?"

"You might say that."

"They were testing you. They do that with all new sitters. I'll speak to them tomorrow."

"No, don't. It'll only make it worse. Becky hates me already."

"What happened?" she asked, lifting her head from his chest.

"Oh, it was nothing serious. Just a little disagreement about bedtime. But she sure didn't like being disciplined by me. I don't think we'll be friends anymore."

"It's a tough balance between being a friend and being a parent." She rested her head back on his chest.

"Parent." Michael tried the word quietly on his lips.

"What?"

"Oh, nothing." He relaxed, holding Jenny in his arms. "I told Lisa a bedtime story."

"Oh yeah? Which one?"

"I just made one up. My mother used to tell me stories. She'd make up these stories with a little religious moral at the end of them. Funny, I never thought about it before tonight. But I think those stories had some kind of subliminal influence on me, moving me back to the church and where I am now."

"You never know." she said, sleepily. "You plant a seed ..."

And with that, she was asleep.

CHAPTER SIXTEEN

now

"Look what we've got!"

The girls burst through the front door carrying little boxes with air holes in them.

"Uh oh." Michael thought to himself. "This can't be good."

"Michael, Michael. Look what we've got." Lisa crashed into Michael, who was sitting on a chair in the living room. Becky was not far behind her. Gerald and Mildred lagged behind, with sheepish looks on their faces. Anita stood behind them.

"What's in the boxes, girls?" he asked, dreading the answer.

"We got guinea pigs!" Lisa announced.

"They're not guinea pigs, goofus." Becky corrected. "They're hamsters."

"Is there a difference?" Michael asked, not really caring about an answer.

"I dunno." Lisa said.

"I hope you don't mind, Michael." Mildred approached cautiously. "I know we should have asked first. But the girls were so excited. And they said they never had a pet before."

"They told you that?" Michael's face tensed up. He looked at the girls, still holding onto their innocent faces. "What about Jedidiah? Did you forget we have a cat? Speaking of which, where is that darned cat? He's always disappearing."

"Cats aren't pets." Becky reasoned. "They're part of the family."

"What are we supposed to do with these hamsters?" Michael complained.

"Love them." Lisa answered simply.

Both girls opened their boxes to take out their new pets.

"Don't let them out!" Michael protested. "They'll run away and poop all over the place."

"No they won't." Becky said.

"You said 'Poop'." Lisa giggled.

"We bought a cage for the hamsters, Michael." Mildred offered. "Gerald, go back out to the car and bring the cage in."

"Yes dear." Gerald retreated out the door.

"If it's a problem, we can keep them with us, Michael." Mildred said.

Michael's thoughts raced. Was this a ploy to get the girls to come stay with them? It was certainly a play to win the girls' affections. Mildred was starting to get on his nerves.

Gerald came back in, carrying a large cage, along with some hamster food and a bag of straw.

"Here you go." He said, dropping his load on the floor in front of Michael.

"I suppose you have names for them already?" he said, looking at the girls, who were holding the hamsters close to their chests.

"This is Gingerbread." Becky answered, holding the hamster toward Michael's face. "See, she's brown – like gingerbread."

"Mine's Miss Piggy." Lisa held her hamster tight. "'Cause she's a guinea pig."

"She's not a guinea pig, Lisa." Becky said sharply. "I told you, she's a hamster."

"I don't care." Lisa was unfazed. "I like the name 'Miss Piggy'."

"Well, Miss Piggy sort of fits." Michael offered to blank stares. "You know – ham and pig? Pig and ham – ster? Get it?"

"What do pigs have to do with ham?" Becky asked.

"You know, it's, well, never mind. Where do you plan on keeping these hamsters?" Michael asked, changing the subject.

"In my room." Becky answered.

"No, my room." Lisa stomped her foot.

"Maybe we should have gotten two cages." Mildred said.

"No, they need to stay together so they can keep each other company." Becky responded, and Lisa nodded in agreement.

"Okay, I guess we can put them in the hallway between your rooms." Michael said, resigning himself to the new additions to the household. "At least for now."

"I think that's an excellent suggestion." Anita offered, seemingly from out of nowhere.

"Thank you, Michael, for letting the girls keep the hamsters." Mildred said.

"Yeah, sure. Only, Mildred, please, no more surprises, okay?"

"No, of course not, Michael." she said sweetly.

"Uh, honey, I think there's something else we need to tell him." Gerald moved over to his wife.

Michael groaned silently. What now?

"Oh yes, you're right, dear." Mildred clasped her hands together as she looked at Michael. "Michael, I suppose we should let you know that we've left the hotel we've been staying at."

"Oh?"

"Yes, we're renting a house nearby here. We figured as long as we're going through this we should have more of a home atmosphere for the girls – for when they come to visit."

"Visit?"

Anita stepped out from the background. "Yes, Mr. Griggs. This seemed like a logical next step, to allow the girls to spend quality time with their grandparents away from this house. Again, I'll be supervising."

Michael felt himself lose control of his body. This was too much to take in.

"And how soon are you proposing these visits?" he asked, numbly.

"Soon. In fact ..." Anita let her sentence go unfinished.

Mildred stepped in to complete the thought.

"We were thinking that the girls could spend Thanksgiving vacation with us. You'd be welcome to join us for Thanksgiving Dinner, of course."

Michael's face whitened, as the blood rushed out.

"Michael?" Mildred looked for a response.

"Mr. Griggs?" Anita looked for a sign of life, as she waved her hand in front of Michael's face.

"You'll have to excuse me." Michael said, as he slowly got out of the chair. "This is all too much to take in right now." His feet were wobbly as he made his way out of the room.

"Well, I think that went well." Mildred looked at her husband. "Don't you, dear?"

Gerald shook his shoulders. Becky and Lisa continued petting their hamsters. Anita looked around the room, haplessly.

CHAPTER SEVENTEEN

then

As the months moved forward, Michael and Jenny rapidly became a part of each other's lives. They no longer dated. They were just always together. Michael began being included in the Friday Family Pizza Night. Lisa accepted it naturally, but Becky seemed to resent it at first. However, soon she too accepted his presence as part of the family.

Summertime came quickly upon them. Things slowed down around the church during the summer months, leaving the couple more time to spend together. But summer also began a painful countdown. Michael's internship would end in August and he would have to return to Gettysburg for his final year of seminary. They were both keenly aware of how short their remaining time together was, but neither of them discussed it. Instead, they chose to make the most of each day they had together.

As Michael's last week in New Jersey approached, silent moments replaced the casual summer conversations. There was only one topic on both their minds, and each was about to explode from the torturous silence. Finally, Jenny spoke.

"You know we have to talk about this." she said after another long silence, as the two of them sat on the front steps of her house.

"About what?" He did not look at her. Instead, he kept his attention focused on the darkening sky as the sun set beneath a purple tinged cloud.

"What we haven't talked about all summer." she continued. "You're leaving in five days."

"I know. It's all I've been thinking about." He continued to look out as the purple sky turned dark gray.

Jenny stumbled for words. "I just want to say ... it's been really great, wonderful, knowing you. You've changed my life."

He could hear the tiny sobs being choked back in her words. He turned his head to face her. It was hard to see her eyes in the dim light. He tried to put his arm around her.

"Just let me finish this." she said, taking his arm away and holding his hand in both of hers. "I don't ... regret anything. I'm so glad you came into my life. But, but ... I don't expect anything of you. I know you'll be going back to Pennsylvania and your friends. I just don't want you to think that I'm ... I don't want to hold you back. What I'm saying is ... I'll be all right. You've got a great life ahead of you, and I've got my life here. But the sooner we stop thinking about each other and get on with our lives, the better off we'll be. So maybe we should end it right now and start getting used to living without each other again. It won't be easy forgetting you, but I want you to be able to forget about me without any guilt."

"What are you talking about?" There was both fear and anger in his voice as he pulled his hand away from hers. "I don't want to forget about you. And I don't want you to forget about me. What did you think, I was just going to drive out of here and leave everything we had together behind?"

"It's probably for the best."

"You're crazy!" Michael's anger was coming to the fore.

"Please don't be mad at me. I don't want you to go away mad. I'm just afraid. It's so hard being alone. You opened a place in my heart, and I'm afraid of the painful loneliness I'll feel when you're gone. I've already been feeling it for weeks, and I'm trying to prepare myself for when you go." Jenny was openly crying now.

Michael's anger subsided. "Wait here a minute." he said, getting up.

"Where are you going? You're not leaving now, are you?"

"No, I'm just going to my car. I'll be right back."

Michael opened the back door of his car and pulled out a large cardboard box. He brought it back to the steps.

"This is for you." he said, placing the box down by Jenny's side. "I was thinking about how I'd have to be leaving soon, so I went out today and bought this for you."

Jenny looked at the beat-up box. She noticed the air holes right away.

"What did you do?" she asked, a softness coming over her face.

She quickly opened the box and pulled out a little white furred kitten.

"It's not a real Persian." Michael said softly. "But it's the closest thing I could find."

"You remembered." Jenny rubbed the kitten across her face.

"I got him so you won't forget me. He can keep you company until I come back. Are you going to name it Snowball II?"

"No, I'm going to call him Jedidiah."

"Jedidiah?" he asked, puzzled. "That's an odd name for a cat."

"Jedidiah means 'loved by the Lord'. Second Samuel 12."

"Wow, I'm impressed."

"I was just reading that part of the Bible this morning. I came across the name and its meaning, and I liked it. So I remembered it."

"I didn't know you read the Bible."

"Uh huh. Especially when I'm sad. It gives me comfort." She placed the kitten down in the box and continued to rub its back. "Jedidiah. Loved by the Lord and loved by me ... because he'll always make me think of you."

Michael sat down on the other side of the box. "Uh, I got something else for you too. I bought it last week and I've been waiting for the right time to give it to you."

He reached into his shirt pocket and pulled out a delicate gold chain necklace holding a small gold heart with diamond chips in it.

"Oh, it's so beautiful." she said, clutching it to her breast. She then opened her hand and gazed at the heart. "Help me put it on, please."

Michael got up and Jenny stood and handed him the necklace.

"Before I put this on, I have to explain something." he said, as she looked into his eyes. "I really wanted to buy you an engagement ring. I went looking, but I couldn't afford one. This necklace was the one thing of my mother's that I've held onto all these years. I was saving it for something special. So this is a sort of engagement necklace. I hope it's all right."

Jenny looked down and started to cry. She held the necklace tightly to her breast again.

"So how about it?" he asked. "Will you marry me?"

CHAPTER EIGHTEEN

then

"**Y**es."
Pushing aside Jedidiah's box, she wrapped her arms around Michael's neck and buried her face in his chest, crying gently.

He found tears forming in his own eyes. A combination of relief and sheer happiness broke the tension that had been building up inside. For the first time in a long time he felt a true sense of peace within, telling him that all was right.

"I was so afraid you'd say no." he said, looking out into the night. "And then after you started talking about forgetting each other ..."

She pulled back her head to face him. "I'm sorry. I was just so afraid of being hurt again. I started putting up that shield that I've grown so good at building. But everything's going to be all right now, isn't it?"

"Yes. It's going to be great."

Jenny arched her back, as a look of sobriety came over her face.

"We've got so much to do before you leave. So many plans to make, so many arrangements. Oh, Michael, I can hardly believe this is all real. It is real, isn't it? You're not just trying to let me down easy? You're not going to disappear and forget about me?"

"No. Will you stop that?"

"I'm sorry. I'm sorry. I'd understand, you know. I'd hate you, but I'd understand."

"You're driving me nuts. I just asked you to marry me. I want to spend the rest of my life with you."

She placed her fingers gently on his lips. "Oh, I do so love you. Don't mind me. I think nervousness is taking over. But it's better being nervous than afraid. Or alone."

Jenny again wrapped her arms around Michael's neck, placing her cheek against his. Then she moved to kiss him. They spent several moments hugging and kissing one another, holding on to the magic in the night.

"I can't wait to tell the girls." she said finally, relinquishing the time-held moment. "They'll be so happy."

Michael did not respond.

Jenny wondered about his blank, outward gaze. "What about your father? What will he say?"

"Oh, I've got a pretty good idea." he said, still looking into the distance. "But I don't really care. He doesn't approve of a lot of the things I do."

"Because I'm divorced." she said in a low, sad voice.

"You have to understand, it's not you. He's just that way about things. But he got remarried after my mother died. He should understand that a person has a right to be happy. And if he doesn't, too bad."

Michael looked at Jenny and saw the sadness in her face, despite the night masking a clear view. He searched for something positive to say.

"You know, though, my mother would really like you. She'd be happy for us."

"You never talk much about your mother. But I can tell her death affected you deeply. Jenny paused before asking, "How did she die?"

Michael now paused before answering.

"It was an auto accident." he said softly, looking down. "A drunken driver hit her. Nothing ever happened to him." The bitterness in his voice was tangible. "He never even said he was sorry. He didn't even remember anything that happened. Such a jerk. I think that's why I never drank. It's just too stupid."

They spent a few moments in silence staring into the night sky, now filled with stars. Jenny finally gently interrupted the silence.

"My father died of cancer. I think I told you that." She paused again in thought. "It was awful. He lasted for a year and a half in great pain. My mother had to give him morphine for the pain. But in the end it didn't help much. They put him in the hospital and he just wasted away. Now my mother's cancer came quick. By the time it was diagnosed there wasn't much that they could do. She was gone before they even came up with a plan for treatment."

Jenny took a tissue from her pocket to wipe her nose.

"I hope I don't linger." she said, tearing at the tissue with her hands. "I don't want to die in a hospital, either. I want to die at home. And after I'm gone, I want a simple service, not some big show. And not in a funeral home, not in a church. It would be too sad. Just a short graveside service."

The quiet was palpable. Then, suddenly, Jenny jumped up from the steps.

"Hey, what are we doing talking about death?" New energy powered her voice. "We've got a wedding to talk about."

Clutching Jedidiah in one hand, Jenny took Michael's hand and led him inside. They spent the rest of the evening in one another's arms, saying little, holding onto the moment.

There was much to be done and talked about before Michael headed back to complete his final year of seminary. Details were quickly fleshed out. Rather than upset the girls' lives so abruptly, the wedding would wait until Michael graduated. Jenny would stay in New Jersey with the girls, and after graduation they would move the family to Pennsylvania, where Michael would seek a call to a congregation.

One joyful task was taken care of right away. The next morning Jenny and Michael happily broke the news of their future plans to Lisa and Becky. Neither of them anticipated the girls' reactions.

"No, Mommy. You can't marry him."

Jenny was shocked by Lisa's adamancy. She had never seen her like this before.

"Lisa, what's wrong? Why are you acting like this?"

The little girl was in tears, shouting, "He's not a part of our family. Why do you want to be with him?"

Jenny knelt down and tried to calm Lisa down.

"I love Michael. And he loves me. We want to be together. And Michael loves you too, both of you. We'll all be a family together."

"No. I don't want him. I want you. Tell him to go away."

Michael stood in the background, too numb to respond. Lisa's words hurt him deeply. Jenny was clearly shaken, but was doing her best to deal with the situation.

"Lisa, he's not going away. I'm not going away either. I'll always be with you. That won't change."

"No. You'll go away too. You'll want to be with him instead."

"But Lisa, you like Michael."

Lisa's voice came down an octave. "Yes."

"Then wouldn't it be nice if Michael could be with us all the time?"

"No, I don't want things to change."

Jenny looked over at Becky, who had stood quietly throughout Lisa's outburst.

"And what about you? What do you think of the idea?"

Becky spoke softly, but matter-of-factly. "I like the way things are now. Why can't we stay together and just have him come and visit sometimes like he does now?"

Jenny stood up. Her voice was quivering. "I can't believe this. After everything I've been through, don't I deserve some happiness in my life? Why can't you be happy for me?"

She ran upstairs into her bedroom. Her crying could be heard from the living room. Michael stood motionless, not knowing what to do. Lisa's tears started up again and she ran off to her room. Becky looked deeply into Michael's eyes.

"You've really messed up everything." she said plainly before retreating to her room.

Michael stood alone in the living room, unable to move, wishing he had a bedroom to run off to.

He approached the bedroom door gingerly and peered in. Jenny was lying across the bed on her stomach, softly sobbing into her pillow. He slowly sat down upon the bed. Jenny sat up and quietly buried her head into his chest.

She spoke softly, calmly, a slight sniffle in her voice. "Why can't things be easy? Why can't it ever be simple?"

Without thinking, Michael kept repeating, "I know. I know."

"It's going to be all right, you know." she said, strangely confident. "I'll talk to them. They'll adjust. We're going to be happy."

"I know. I know."

Jenny looked up and stared into his eyes.

"No, really. It's going to be okay. I can feel it." There was a positive determination in her words.

"I believe you." But Michael wasn't sure he did.

"I don't know what it is, but suddenly I know everything is right. It's like God is reassuring me. I can feel it inside. I'm going to talk to them right now. It's all going to work out."

She jumped out of the bed and went to the dresser mirror to clear the tears from her face.

"Should I go with you?" Michael asked.

"No. I think it's better if you just went home first. Let me talk to them alone. It'll be a good Mother/Daughter talk. You just go home. Don't worry. Leave it all to me."

"Are you sure?"

"Yes." she said, escorting him out of the room and down the stairs. "You go ahead. I'll give you a call later."

He was reassured by the confidence in her voice. Whatever happened to change her mood was obviously a good sign. Michael felt better about leaving things in Jenny's hands.

Jenny led him to the door and gave him a gentle kiss goodbye. As Michael walked toward his car, he heard Jenny speak softly, "I love you, Michael." The words carried him all the way home.

◆◆◆

The last few days were hard. Jenny and Michael spent as much time together as possible. An uneasy truce was worked out with the girls. They kept their opinions about the wedding plans to themselves, but Michael could see in their faces that they resented his intrusion into the stable mix they had grown up with.

Finally, the last day came, and, when he could hold off no longer, Michael drove off in his packed car, heading for Pennsylvania, while Jenny stood in the street watching the car fade into the distance. She prayed silently that she was not watching her future fading away.

The next nine months were difficult for the both of them, yet it also served to strengthen their commitment to each other and their future together. Expenses were tight, keeping Michael and Jenny apart for long stretches of time. They survived on letters and phone calls. Occasionally, Jenny was able to get a free weekend from work. Leaving the girls with her neighbor, she would arrive at the seminary late on a Friday evening. Saturday was their day to be together, to be in love, to share dreams, and plan for after graduation. Sunday mornings Jenny would join Michael as he supply preached at a nearby church in Littlestown to earn some extra money. Then she was on her way back home, giving Michael some time to study. After Jenny's visits, Michael's mind was never focused on studying. The time was far too short. But neither of them would give up a moment of it.

Michael was only able to come back to New Jersey once, on Christmas. It was the only time he had seen or talked to the girls in the entire nine months. He had almost forgotten that the girls existed. In a way, it was an escape from having to deal with the whole picture of his impending marriage. Not only was he going to be a husband, but his marriage would make him an instant father. No sane man would make such a commitment knowing the full ramifications of his decision. It was better to walk in unawares.

Reality was brought home to Michael on Graduation Day. Jenny brought the girls with her to witness the graduation ceremonies the second week of May. He had already introduced Jenny to his friends. They knew that he was engaged. But no mention was ever made of the girls. Now Michael found himself introducing Becky and Lisa as his soon-to-be stepdaughters. The stunned looks received from his friends were having a sobering effect on Michael. Just graduated and already a family man. He felt the weight of the chain around his leg dragging whenever he moved.

But then he would look into her face. Jenny's smile, her total beauty, shone through any doubts or concerns. It was great having her there to share this important moment of his life, especially since none of his own family felt the need to attend. The truth was now sinking in. Jenny was now his family. Jenny and her two little girls.

❖❖❖

Graduation turned out to be the breather before the whirlwind events of the next few weeks. Graduation was on a Wednesday. The wedding was set for that Saturday. Jenny had made all the arrangements. Michael removed himself from the process, partly due to distance and partly due to personal preference.

The service was held at Lord of Love, with Eric presiding. Being her second marriage, Jenny kept things simple. Becky was Maid of Honor and Lisa was Flower Girl. Michael's friend, Lee, served as Best Man.

Michael arrived in Holmdel on Friday and checked into a hotel. It was unusually cold for May. He talked to Jenny on the phone, but, in keeping with tradition, he did not see her before the ceremony. Michael's family drove in for the wedding and were staying at the same hotel. They spent Friday evening in the hotel lounge listening to some local singer performing protest songs from the Sixties. Some bachelor party, he thought to himself. He and his sister spent most of the night sitting in a corner, talking about raising children. Not terribly exciting, but Michael appreciated Julie's advice and calming effect on him, nonetheless.

He got out of bed early Saturday morning, unable to get much sleep. He went to the window in the room and peered through the curtain. It was an awful, gray day. The sky was full of threatening clouds. "I hope it doesn't rain." he said quietly.

He took a shower, then checked his watch. "Only 7:30. Five and a half hours before show time." Too soon to get dressed, he thought. But what else was there to do? He put on his jeans and a sweatshirt and went out for a walk. The cold wind chilled his still wet hair and tore through his sweatshirt. He didn't mind. He needed the sensation to clear his head. His thoughts were a jumble. On the one side was the awesome responsibility of marriage and family. On the other side was Jenny. That was the side that kept winning out. The thought of her always being beside him, supporting him, and being his partner made everything else seem inconsequential. They could face anything and everything – together. For the first time, Michael fully realized that this was the one thing he had always wanted, the one thing he had always been looking for, all his life. With his senses cleared, suddenly Michael felt hungry.

He had breakfast at a nearby diner. He noted that he was the only one there sitting alone. That's the way it had always been for him. He never minded being alone. For him, it was the way to survive through life. Now that was about to change, forever. As the check came, he took another look at his watch. The countdown was now at four hours. He went back to his room and got changed.

He arrived at the church over an hour early. He figured he could kill some time catching up with Eric. But Eric was not there yet. Michael's family was still at the hotel getting ready. He looked around for Lee. He was supposed to meet him at the church. "I hope he doesn't get lost." he said to the air. He sat in his old office and waited.

It was now 12:30. "Less than a half hour now." he thought. "I sure hope Lee gets here soon."

Some of the guests began arriving. Michael moved over to Eric's office to wait. Eric arrived at the church, but was too busy to talk.

"Your hair's wet." Michael said to him.

"Yeah, it's starting to rain." Eric replied casually.

"Oh no!" Michael thought, thinking of Jenny. He knew she was having her hair done that morning. He went to an exit door to take a look out. It was no longer raining. It was snowing – hard.

"May! This is May! It's not supposed to snow in May. What in the world is going on?"

Big flakes were coming down fast. There was already accumulation on the ground. Guests were coming in soaked, with squishy shoes. By the time one o'clock came around, the walkway from the parking lot was covered in snow. Michael saw Jenny's limousine coming into the parking lot and it pulled up to the walkway. The rear window slid down slightly and Michael could hear Jenny's voice cry out, "Help!"

He grabbed a nearby broom and rushed out in his tuxedo to clear the walkway. His rented shoes were ruined. Jenny came out of the car, wrapped her wedding gown inside her raincoat, and made a dash for the entrance, with Becky and Lisa running in behind her. She was laughing. Michael was relieved. By the time she got inside, her hair was a mess. She spent some time in the bathroom trying to fix it. Michael waited, his nervousness becoming more prominent. Becky and Lisa waited outside the bathroom, both looking very cute in their new white dresses, despite the frowns on their faces. Lee was a no-show. Michael only found out several weeks later that he had opted to attend a Paul McCartney concert in New York City instead.

Jenny came out of the bathroom, radiant in spite of her wet, wrinkled gown and matted down hair. Her smile was still perfect. And that was good enough for him. He couldn't believe she was holding up so well.

Sensing Michael's concern, she said, "Hey, look, my first wedding was a gorgeous, sunny day. And that didn't work out so great. This time I've got you, and that's all that matters to me. And you know we'll always remember this wedding day."

As she headed off to her position to walk down the aisle, she added, "This will give us something to laugh about in our old age."

She stood at the back of the sanctuary, a picture of composure. The organist began 'The Wedding March'. Jenny looked back at Michael, still standing by the bathroom.

"Are you ready?" she asked.

Michael nodded.

"Well, what are you waiting for?" she motioned for him to move. "Get in there. Let's get this show on the road."

Michael gladly complied.

It was a beautiful ceremony, despite Michael's inability to repeat the vows correctly. The reception was held in the church's Fellowship Hall. Everyone from the church was invited, and cake and punch were served. By four o'clock all the guests had gone and Michael and Jenny were ready to hit the road. It had stopped snowing. Now it was pouring rain.

The girls had already left with their neighbor, with whom they would spend the week while their mother and Michael were on their honeymoon. Jenny had picked the honeymoon location – Cape Cod.

CHAPTER NINETEEN

now

It was yet another restless night. The girls were spending Thanksgiving vacation with their grandparents. He had reluctantly joined them for the Thanksgiving feast, forcing a smile through most of the meal. Then he came back home – alone.

He had learned by now that if sleep wasn't coming, he might as well get up and do something useful. This time he went out to the garage and began sorting through more of Jenny's things. He had started many times before, but never got very far. The memories just became too painful for him to continue. But also, in a strange way, he found some comfort in the process. It brought back some good memories. And he was learning things about Jenny that he never knew before.

As he looked through a box containing some notebooks and other mementos from Jenny's high school days he came across a piece of paper tucked loosely in one of the notebooks. The paper had obviously been torn out from the same notebook. But it wasn't from her high school days. It was a poem. And on the top Jenny had printed out her name. Jennifer Farley Griggs. The word 'Farley' had been crossed out, as if Jenny had forgotten at first that she had a new married name, and then corrected it. There was a date next to it. It had been written shortly after their honeymoon, right about the time Jenny had received her diagnosis. Michael read the words on the page.

God Made the Rainbow

Looking out over the water
the ocean seems so vast.
I take in this moment
hoping it will last.

Some days seem so long,
sometimes things go wrong.
But I keep looking out to sea
knowing God is watching me.

He has made a promise
that I know He'll keep.
And I find my peace
in His love so deep.

So now I sit here staring
searching the rainy skies.
I know it's out there somewhere,
it's where my hope lies.

Troubles seem to come and go,
but it will be all right.
No matter how dark the night
this one thing I know –

God made the rainbow.

As he studied the words, it felt like a key had suddenly unlocked the door that was keeping him from reaching that nagging thought in his head that had been keeping him up for so many nights. He had been looking for an answer. Only he didn't even know the question. He was trying to recover a memory that wouldn't come because he didn't know where to look. But now he knew. His thoughts raced back to their honeymoon on Cape Cod.

CHAPTER TWENTY

then

They spent the night at a nearby hotel. Early the next morning they were on their way to Truro, near the end of the Cape. It was still cold for May and the clouds were sticking around, but at least it had stopped raining – and snowing.

They stopped in Connecticut along the way for lunch in the little town of Mystic. After lunch, they strolled through Mystic Village, checking out the quaint shops and buying little souvenirs for the girls. Michael wanted to buy a shark in a bottle for Becky, but Jenny didn't think she'd appreciate it. They settled on a Troll doll for each of the girls from a Scandinavian store instead. Michael was thoroughly enjoying every moment, as was Jenny. No one walking by needed more than one glance to see that they were in love. They walked along, holding hands, stopping every so often in front of a picturesque scene and asking a passerby to take a picture of the two of them together. Usually, Jenny sat on Michael's lap for the picture, though Michael was on Jenny's lap for the photo by the duck pond. The skies began clearing and it felt nice out in the sun. Michael wanted to spend some time over at Mystic Seaport down the road, but Jenny was anxious to get to the Cape.

They arrived in Truro a little before five. The New England sky was overcast and gray. Jenny was driving and she knew just where she was going. They pulled into the Jackrabbit Cottage Community located within some woods. Michael waited in the car while Jenny checked in at the main office. She was in charge. Soon, they were settling into their little cottage.

It was small - or 'cozy', as Jenny described it, but nice. There was one open room with a kitchenette and dining table, and a couch and chair facing a stone fireplace. The walls were all authentic wood paneling. Beside a tiny bathroom, there was one small bedroom. It was home for the next week.

After unpacking, Michael was feeling hungry.

"I guess we should find some place to eat for dinner, and then buy some groceries later."

"Yeah, sure." Jenny said. "But first, we have to go over and check out the beach."

She already had her jacket on to head out.

"Right now?" he protested. "My stomach's growling. We've got all week to hang out at the beach."

Jenny wrapped her arms around Michael and put on her little girl face, matched with her little girl's voice.

"Ple-e-e-ase, Michael. I've been looking forward to this for so long. I want to walk on the beach. Just for a little while?"

"You act like you've never seen a beach before. They have beaches in New Jersey, you know."

"Oh, but not like Cape Cod beaches. There's nothing around but sand and ocean for miles and miles. And dunes. Wonderfully tall dunes. No boardwalks. No arcades. No pollution. Just God's creation in all its majesty. Oh, I can't wait. Let's go! Let's go!"

She was out the door before he could say anything. So he grabbed his coat and followed behind.

It was a short drive to the beach, less than five minutes. Jenny leapt out of the car and ran down the dune to greet the ocean.

Michael stood in the parking lot at the edge of the dune, looking down. It was about a 20 foot drop from the parking lot to sea level. It was almost a straight drop, but there was a path worn into the sand dune leading down the side. It didn't look to be too hard going down, but he wondered how anybody was able to climb back up. He watched as Jenny reached the level area of the beach. There looked to be about 50 feet of beach before meeting the ocean. Michael wondered if it was low tide. Jenny had already reached the water. She had tossed her shoes on the beach and was dancing with the waves. It didn't look like she was coming back any time soon. He decided to climb down.

"Isn't this great!" she said excitedly, as Michael approached.

"It looks awfully cold." he said, countering her excitement.

"Oh yes it is. It's wonderful." She continued running back and forth, playing tag with the ocean. "Take your shoes off. Join the fun."

"That's all right. I'll just watch."

He sat down on the sand. He could feel the cold sand through his pants. He placed his hand down and let the cool sand sift through his fingers. He had to admit that it felt kind of nice.

The sun had set behind the clouds, leaving a dull evening light. The whitecaps of the waves were glistening against the shaded darkness. Despite the ocean's beauty, he couldn't take his eyes off of Jenny. He had never seen her looking so lovely. And she always looked lovely to him. But now was something special. It was as if he were seeing the real Jenny for the first time. Maybe not so much real as *full*. This was Jenny at her peak, the free-spirited child unencumbered by the responsibility of parenthood and the weight of life's cruelties. This was the image of her that he wanted to remember forever.

Jenny ran over and jumped into his arms, knocking them both back into the sand. She kissed him passionately.

"I love you." she whispered.

Just as quickly, she was back on her feet and ready to keep moving.

"Let's go for a walk." she suggested. Her feet were already leading her down the beach.

"I thought we were going to get something to eat." he protested, uselessly. She was already on her way. He ran to catch up to her.

For the first time, he noticed how expansive the coastline was. He took a look behind him. For as far as he could see, in either direction, there was nothing but sandy beach, bordered by the ocean on one side and rising dunes on the other side. He couldn't help being impressed by the vastness of it all. But reality soon got the better of him.

"Jenny, it's starting to get awfully dark. I think we should turn around before it gets too dark to see."

He expected another protest, but to his surprise Jenny agreed.

"I'm hungry." she said simply. "Let's get dinner."

They walked back toward the parking lot hand in hand.

They had dinner in a quiet little restaurant in town overlooking the bayside of Truro. Except for one other older couple, they had the restaurant to themselves. It was too early in the season for the summer tourist trade, when the town would be overrun by visitors looking for a shore vacation. Jenny liked it this way – quiet, uncrowded. Michael had to agree.

The rest of the evening was spent quietly at the cottage. Michael built a fire in the fireplace, a first-time experience for him. He knew nothing about chimney flues, so the room quickly filled with smoke. Jenny quickly rectified the situation and they opened the windows to air out the room. They then sat in a cuddling embrace on the couch, saying little, watching the flames spark and crackle. When the fire died out, they tiredly retreated into the bedroom.

The sun poured into the small bedroom early the next morning - too early for Michael. He reached over for Jenny. But she wasn't there. He dragged himself out into the main room. The smell of coffee permeated the room, replacing the smell of smoke from the previous evening. But Jenny was still nowhere to be found inside. He looked out the front door. Jenny was sitting on the porch, legs up on the bench, coffee mug in hand.

"Good morning." she said, looking his way.

"Mmm." he mumbled.

"You know," she said seriously, "that's a bad habit of yours I've noticed."

"What?"

"You hardly ever say casual greetings like 'Hello' or 'Goodbye', at least to me. I don't think I've ever heard you say 'Good Morning' or 'Goodnight'."

Michael thought about it for a moment.

"That's an exaggeration. But I guess you're right." he admitted, slowly. "I guess it's just the way I grew up. We were never much for greetings in my family."

"Well we're going to have to change that, Mister."

"What, we're married for two whole days and already you're trying to change me?"

"I'm serious. We're a family now. Becky and Lisa are used to hellos and goodbyes. You'd better get used to it too."

"Yes ma'am." He half-saluted. "But if I'm going to have to change, you're going to have to change some things as well."

"Like what?" she asked, a concerned look on her face.

"Well, I can't think of anything right now."

She was perfect just the way she was. But he didn't want to admit that to her at that moment.

"What are you doing out here?" he asked, changing the subject.

"Just listening and breathing." she answered, taking a sip of coffee. "Smell the pine. Isn't it great?"

Michael took a deep breath to appreciate the scent of the pine trees all around them.

"That's nice. Very nice. What are you listening to?" he asked.

"Oh, the birds, the crickets, the ocean in the distance. But mostly the silence." She paused. "It's a beautiful morning. It's going to be a beautiful day. The sun is out, the sky is clear. It's warming up. Summer's on its way."

She took a deep breath and stretched out her arms, as if embracing the elements around her.

"Don't you just love the summer?" she said in a wistful tone. "The sunshine and warm weather, the beach. Everything's so green."

"Well, actually, I'm allergic to summer."

"What an old poop you are. Come on, sit down beside me." she said, bringing her legs down and patting the open space on the bench. "Allergic to summer, indeed."

They sat together in silence. For a moment it felt like time had stopped. The world was waiting patiently until they were ready to proceed.

"What do you want to do today?" she asked, after a few minutes had gone by.

Michael breathed in.

"Well, we never did find a grocery store last night. I suppose we should take care of that so that we don't spend all our money on restaurants." He paused. "We should probably find some place to get breakfast first, though. Then after that, maybe we could take a drive around and do some exploring. How does that sound to you?"

"Good." she said without emotion. Then, more enthusiastically she added, "But do you think maybe first we could stop off at the beach?"

◆◆◆◆◆◆

Their week on the Cape was spent doing many things – trips into Provincetown to walk through the town and check out the little shops, quiet walks through the woods, exploring the towns of Truro and nearby Wellfleet, and romantic evenings in their rented cottage. But the centerpiece of the week was always the ocean. Jenny never tired of going to the beach. Early mornings, mid-days, and late evenings were spent there. At times, it was warm enough for Jenny to splash around in the water. Other times, they took long walks along the vast stretches of coastline. Sometimes they just parked at the edge of the parking lot and looked out at the never-ending waves. Although Michael did not share her love for the ocean, he stood in wonder at the joy it brought out in Jenny.

They were walking along the warm, noonday sand, picking up shells and brightly colored pebbles that caught their fancy. Suddenly, Michael found himself walking alone. He turned around to see Jenny standing still, looking out over the water. It was something he was beginning to get used to. He walked back to join her.

"What is it about you and this ocean?" he said, as a throw-away line coming up to her, not really expecting an answer.

"Just look out there." she replied, her gaze still focused outward. "Look as far as you can see. Strain your eyes to their limit. Try to find the farthest point. What do you see?"

"I see … water. Water and the sky."

"I see eternity." she said evenly, never letting her gaze slip. "No matter how far I can see, the ocean goes beyond my limited vision. It's infinite. And I'm only finite."

"So you like feeling small?" he said, not really understanding the feeling behind her words.

"But I don't feel small. I feel … real. I have a place. I fit into a space made just for me by God."

Michael changed his gaze from the ocean to Jenny's profile.

"I … don't think I follow you." he said, taking notice that she was sharing something important with him.

Jenny sat down on the sand. Michael sat down next to her.

"When I look out there" she began, still staring out, "and see where the ocean and sky seem to meet, these two great eternal bodies coming together, it represents to me the movement of life. The sky goes on forever, and the ocean goes on forever, both constantly moving and changing, and both changing the world they encounter. But here they come together, as if they have a purpose in meeting.

That tells me that life has a purpose. And so does everything in it, including me. Someone had to make it that way. God."

She paused only briefly to take a deep breath before continuing.

"When I see the ocean, I see God at work. It tells me God is real, and that makes me feel real. It's like the whole cosmos suddenly clicks into place, giving everything meaning. And that gives me a good feeling about myself. I know there's a reason for my being here, even if I don't know what that reason is."

For the first time, she looked at Michael, catching him staring at her.

"Does that make me sound like a nut job to you?"

"No." he said simply. "No, not at all."

Jenny rested her body against his. They sat in silence for quite some time.

"Maybe we should get going." Michael finally spoke.

"In a little bit." she responded dreamily. "I'm still looking."

"What are you looking for?" he joked.

"Rainbows."

Michael was not expecting an answer. He wasn't sure if she was joking in reply.

"Rainbows?" he questioned.

"Um hm."

Michael's silence seemed to demand further explanation from her.

"I love to look for rainbows over the water. When I was a little girl, I saw my very first rainbow here on this beach. It was just after a quick cloudburst of rain. It looked so beautiful shining over the water. It was the most beautiful thing I had ever seen. I ran over to my father to show him and to ask him what it was. At first, he told me a story about leprechauns and a pot of gold. But I didn't believe him. Then he tried to explain how rainbows were really formed, but I was too young to understand. Then he told me another story about a rainbow. A story from the Bible."

Jenny interrupted her memory for a moment, casting an embarrassed look at Michael.

"But I guess you'd know that story already. Sorry."

"No, that's all right." he said, sorry that she had stopped. "I want to hear you tell it."

"Well, you know it's from the story of Noah."

"Yeah, from the book of Genesis. After Noah and his family got off the ark, God set the rainbow in the sky as a sign that he would never send another catastrophic flood."

"Right. Well, my father told me the whole story. Funny, he wasn't a churchgoer, but he knew his Bible stories. He told me all about the animals and the ark and the flood. I remember being captivated by the story. I loved the part about the animals, but the flood part really scared me. How could the world be so bad, I thought, to make God want to destroy everything? But then my father told me about the rainbow. I was glad there was a happy ending. And having just seen that wonderful rainbow for myself made the story all the more real for me."

They sat a little longer in silence. Finally, Jenny stood up. Michael stood beside her. Jenny took one final long gaze into infinity.

"God made the rainbow as a sign of hope, you know." she said, more to the wind than to Michael. Then she turned to face him. "Whenever I feel overwhelmed by life, I look for the rainbow. No matter how bad things may seem, the rainbow for me is a sign that things will be all right."

She looked into his eyes with that penetrating gaze that Michael was beginning to know so well.

"I just wanted you to know that. It's an important part of who I am. Is that all right?"

Michael looked at her and almost melted away.

"Everything about you is all right with me."

They started up the long dune walkway, supported in each other's arms.

It was their last night on Cape Cod. Tomorrow morning would find them back on the road, heading home to New Jersey. One more night of magic before returning to the real world and getting underway with building a new life together. One more night. There was only one place to spend it. On the beach.

They sat by the last glowing embers of a fire that someone else had built on the beach and abandoned. It didn't provide any real warmth or light, but the smell of the burnt wood mingling in with the salt air was a pleasing odor. It added to the atmosphere of the moment. It was too dark to see the ocean, so they listened to the gentle surf lapping back and forth against the shoreline. Their gaze was cast skyward, as they marveled at the stars filling their line of vision. They felt the cool sand under them. They could taste the salt spray on their lips. All their senses were being treated to a joyous sensation. It was a perfect place to be.

"You know," Michael started softly, "I can see now why you connect this place with God. It's all just so overpowering. Yet you don't feel afraid. You feel at peace."

Jenny smiled.

"It really puts everything into perspective." she said, contentment in her voice. "We like to think of ourselves as being in control of our destinies. We think we know everything and can do anything. But people live and die, just one small speck in the larger scheme of things. Generations will pass away, but the ocean goes on and on. The same stars that our ancestors gazed upon in awe will be seen by our descendants."

"You sound like a philosopher." Michael interjected.

"Are you making fun of me?"

"No, no I'm not. I like listening to you. I'm really impressed. I can tell you've put a lot of thought into this."

"Thank you." she said lightly. "I just hope you remember my words. There might be a test later."

"Believe me, I'm memorizing everything you say."

"Well then, let me continue." She paused. "I don't want you to think that a scene like this makes humankind insignificant."

"No, I know it doesn't."

"Being here like this makes me realize that everyone and everything is precious to God. But no one any more so, or less so, than anyone else. We're as important as the stars. There are millions of them. Every one unique, and every one cared for by God."

Jenny started to laugh.

"Listen to me, teaching theology to the theologian."

"I'd rather listen to you than any of my professors." Michael said, as he stirred the embers with a stick.

"It would be nice if we could stay like this forever." She sighed. "But life goes on. Change is a part of the cycle. Still, it's good to know that the ocean will always be here. There's at least one constant in life."

Michael noticed Jenny suddenly shivering.

"Are you cold?"

"No, an odd chill just ran through me. Very strange."

She stood up. Her demeanor took on a sudden, harder change.

"Well, we can't stay here all night. It's time we moved on." she said, turning to walk away. "Come on, Michael. It's time we got ready for tomorrow."

Michael got up and followed behind her. For some unknown reason, as he was about to come alongside her and put his arm around her, he pulled back, like he was afraid to touch her. Had he known what tomorrow would bring - the doctor appointments, the tests, the pain and suffering his bride was about to endure - he would have held her tight and done his best to never let go of the night.

CHAPTER TWENTY ONE

now

He was sound asleep. For the first time in a long time. It was just after Thanksgiving. The girls were back in their own beds after spending the weekend with their grandparents. Michael slept well, having them back under the same roof. But the peaceful sleep was not to last. A tiny voice was speaking into his ear.

"Michael, Michael."

He reluctantly opened one eye and tried to attain focus on the face so close to him.

"Michael, wake up."

"Becky, what is it? What time is it?" He sat up in the bed, as he opened his other eye and adjusted to the light sneaking in from behind the curtains. His grogginess quickly subsided as he saw the concern in Becky's face.

"I went to say good morning to Gingerbread and Miss Piggy, but Gingerbread's sleeping kinda funny."

"Funny? What do you mean?"

"She's sleeping on her side with one eye open."

"Maybe that's just the way she sleeps. Like the old saying, 'Sleeping with one eye open.'"

"Can you just check on her?"

"Sure, honey. Just give me a moment."

Michael pulled himself out of the bed, his body still not fully awake. He went out to the hallway to check on the hamster, with Becky walking close behind him. He saw Miss Piggy munching on some greens, but Gingerbread was lying still on its side, just as Becky had said. He opened the top of the cage and reached in to touch the dormant hamster. As he rubbed his hand against Gingerbread's back, he felt the stiffness in the body. Gingerbread was clearly dead.

"She's just sleeping, right?" Becky's voice was hopeful, but also scared.

"Oh, honey, no. I hate to say this, but Gingerbread's gone. She died."

"No, she's just sleeping." Becky protested, struggling to keep back the tears.

"I wish that were true, Becky. But it's not. We have to face the truth. We need to take her out of the cage so she doesn't infect Miss Piggy, in case she had something catching."

"Can't we just wait a little while, in case she wakes up?"

"She's not going to wake up, honey."

"Please don't say that. She might be sleeping. Please, let's just wait."

"All right." he agreed, reluctantly. "But let's take Miss Piggy out to be safe."

"Okay." she sniffed.

Michael took Miss Piggy out of the cage and handed her to Becky. Becky held onto her and petted her back, as the animal squeaked in contentment. Michael studied Becky's face. This was going to be a heartbreaking moment for her. It was already a heartbreaking moment for him.

"You know Lisa's going to be up soon and coming out to see Miss Piggy and Gingerbread. We'll have to let her know. And it's better if we tell her before she sees Gingerbread like this, don't you think?"

"Yeah, I guess so. Can I just say goodbye to Gingerbread?"

"Sure, honey. Let me take Miss Piggy and put her in the bathtub while you say goodbye."

Michael took hold of Miss Piggy and walked away. A few minutes later Becky came into the bathroom. They both stood over the bathtub, watching Miss Piggy move about her surroundings. Michael placed his hand on Becky's shoulder. She began to cry. Softly. Quietly. Michael sat on the edge of the bathtub.

"It's okay to cry, baby. It's very sad to lose a pet, even one you've only known a little while."

"I really loved her."

"I know."

"Did you love her?"

Michael gulped. "Sure. She was a very nice hamster."

"Do you think she's in heaven with Mommy?"

"I do." He answered instantly, without hesitation. To his own surprise, he found that there was no hypocrisy in his answer. He actually believed what he was saying. "I bet Mommy is already setting up a new play area for Gingerbread. No more cages. Just a good life from now on."

"How can you be sure?"

"Well, I can't be one hundred percent sure. Nobody can. But that's what faith is all about. Faith tells us that there's a loving God who loves us so much that he sent his son to be with us so that he can bring us back to heaven with him – one day, when we're ready. And when that day comes, we'll not only see God face to face, we'll also be with all those we love, like Mommy and Gingerbread."

Michael tried to process his own words as he spoke them. But it was all flooding in too quickly. God was real. He had to be. For heaven to be real, then God must be real too. And heaven had to be real. There was just no way someone like Jenny wouldn't be rewarded for her faithfulness. Jenny was in heaven. She wasn't lost to him forever. There would come a day when they would be reunited. God was real – and God was a loving God who wants only good things for His children. He had always known that, always felt that. It just got hidden somewhere within his grief. But all at once it came rushing back. Michael felt himself crying.

Suddenly he felt arms around his neck. He hadn't even noticed that Becky had climbed upon his lap and put her arms around him. He patted her back.

"It's okay to be sad, honey." he said, reassuring both Becky and himself. "I get sad too sometimes."

"Will I ever feel better?"

"Sure you will. In time. You know what might help?"

"What?"

"You should look for rainbows."

"Huh?"

"It's something your Mommy taught me. Something I forgot about until just now." Once again, Michael flashed back to Cape Cod. But this time, that nagging, forgotten thought that had been lurking within his subconscious did not elude him.

"Your Mommy liked to look for rainbows."

"Why?"

"It gave her hope. Hope when things weren't going her way. Whenever she saw a rainbow she knew everything would be all right."

"I don't get it."

"Rainbows are a sign from God. God made the rainbow as a promise to people that no matter how bad things may seem, everything would turn out all right in the end."

"That sounds like the story about the boat and all the animals."

"That's right. You know that story?"

"Mmm. Mommy used to tell it to me. Did they have hamsters on that boat?"

"I'm sure they did, honey."

"I miss Gingerbread." Becky said softly. Then she added even more quietly, "I miss Mommy."

"I know, baby. I miss Mommy too."

"And Gingerbread?"

"Yes, I miss Gingerbread too."

"I love you, Daddy."

Michael almost missed it. Did she just call him Daddy? Did she say I love you? Michael felt overcome by sheer bliss. He looked up and said a silent 'Thank You' to God.

"I love you, Becky. Very much."

"And Lisa too?"

"And Lisa too."

"And Miss Piggy?"

"Sure. Why not? And Miss Piggy too."

Becky took her arms away from his neck and looked Michael in the eyes.

"Can we get a new hamster?"

"I guess so. Sure."

"Can we go today?"

It appeared Becky was going to be okay.

CHAPTER TWENTY TWO

now

Once again he found himself in the same room, sitting in the same chair at the same table, with the same people staring back at him. The previous meeting with the Candidacy Committee had taken place on Halloween. Now the Christmas season was fully upon them, with Christmas Eve only two weeks away.

In many ways, he felt like he was living in a rerun. Once again, the ministers on the committee barraged him with a series of theological questions which he answered easily. No one seemed anxious to probe into more personal matters. And this time he felt himself more willing to deal with the personal questions. He was in a much better space – emotionally and spiritually.

It seemed that the panel had at last exhausted their line of questioning. Just as Michael thought he could breathe again, the one lay woman on the committee, Melanie Swan, who had remained silent throughout the proceedings just like the previous time, cleared her throat to speak.

"Mr. Griggs, you've answered all the theological questions quite adeptly. But I have just one question for you, and truthfully, I think it's the only question that really matters. Forgive my bluntness, but we know your story and what you're going through right now. My question is, 'Are you here today because you truly want to serve God as an ordained minister, or are you only doing this in the hopes of retaining custody of your two stepdaughters?'"

The room turned deadly quiet. Half the panel were looking down at their papers on the table like they couldn't bear to look Michael in the face. The other half were staring directly at him, waiting for the answer that would most likely decide his fate.

Michael looked at each of the people sitting across from him. Then he fixed his attention on the woman who had asked the question.

He spoke thoughtfully, deliberately. "First, let me say that I agree with you. You're right. It is the only question that really matters. And it's the one question I've asked myself a number of times. It's been going over and over again in my head. And the honest truth is, I did begin this whole process, this whole thing, only because of my girls. Because of Becky and Lisa. When my wife died I was angry with God. I was angry for quite some time. I did a lot of yelling and screaming, and maybe some cursing. I confronted God with my rage. But I got no answer to my questions. Then there came a point, I can't say for sure when, but there came a time when I stopped believing in God. I felt there was nothing out there. The voice I had relied upon for so much of my life was suddenly silent. That's about where I was when I first initiated this process."

Michael paused, as he took a sip of water to give him a moment to collect his thoughts. "I did do this for my girls. They are everything to me. They're my life. And they've given me a gift, a wonderful gift. They gave me my faith back. It was nothing dramatic. But it was a miracle. The miracle was in their eyes. It was in their laughter. And in their tears. At first, I saw my wife, I saw Jenny in them. And then …, and then I began to see God. How could you look at those two wonderful little girls, so innocent and full of life, and not believe in a loving God? I thank God for them every day, even on those days when I feel like strangling them."

Nervous laughter filtered through the panel members. Mrs. Swan spoke again.

"Forgive me if this sounds indelicate, Mr. Griggs, but I have to ask, how have you dealt with your anger with God over the death of your wife?"

"Well, I'm no longer angry. I still have questions from time to time and I try to listen more patiently for some answers. But I've learned to accept that the answers may not be coming, at least for now. I've accepted my wife's death. I'm not happy about it. I'm still devastated. I miss Jenny. I miss her every day. But I thank God every day as well for giving her to me. Even though the time was all too brief, I wouldn't trade a moment of it for anything. I received so much from Jenny. She was a gift from God. And she gave me two wonderful gifts in Becky and Lisa. Jenny lives on through them. So no, I'm no longer angry with God. Just thankful. So thankful."

Just like the last time, he felt the tears beginning to form. But this time, he did not fight them back.

"Mr. Griggs, Michael." Pastor Sloan spoke. "I think you've answered all of our questions. And on behalf of the committee I want to thank you for being so forthcoming. If you wouldn't mind stepping out of the room for a few minutes so that we committee members can talk, I believe that we can wrap this whole thing up today."

Michael got up and adjourned to the reception area of the building. He sat in one of the chairs and stared at the Christmas tree in the corner. He began thinking about the girls' Christmas lists for Santa. He would need to get himself over to the Mall. Then he thought about his own Christmas list. There was only one thing he wanted – custody of Becky and Lisa. If the Committee didn't approve him, he would find another way to provide security for them. He would do whatever he had to do to make it work out.

His thoughts were interrupted by the receptionist, who told him that the Committee members were ready for him again. He got up, entered the conference room, and took his seat.

"Michael, I'll get right to the point." Pastor Sloan spoke for the Committee members. "You may have noticed that this Committee did not press you as hard on certain issues as we might have. Well, there was a reason for that. You see, we had already pretty much decided before you even came in here the first time that, unless you proved to be a complete – excuse the language – jerk, we were going to approve you to seek a call."

"Huh?" was all he could say, as he thought back on all he had went through.

"When Pastor Nordtveit first contacted me to push for that initial meeting, he spent quite a bit of time going on and on about how special you were. He explained what you were going through, your questioning of your faith. Let me tell you, we've all been there at one point or another in our own faith journeys. But Pastor Nordtveit also told me about the great job you were doing with your late wife's children. He spoke so very highly of you. And as you may know, I think very highly of Eric Nordtveit, as does everyone on this committee. What you may not know is that Pastor Nordtveit not only talked to me at length, he called every member of this committee individually and spoke about you to them."

Michael's mouth was involuntarily open as he tried to take in what Pastor Sloan was telling him.

"You probably already know that Pastor Nordtveit is retiring at the end of this month after 40 years of ministry." Pastor Sloan paused for a moment, as in tribute to Eric's years of service. "He had just one request to make as a sort of retirement gift to him. He asked that you be approved. He said he couldn't think of anyone else as qualified to step into his shoes. So how could we say 'No'? And besides, luckily for you, you didn't turn out to be a jerk. We were all quite impressed by you."

"Thank you." Michael said. "I can't think of anything else, but thank you."

"Of course this all has to go to the Bishop for his final approval," Pastor Sloan continued, "but just as Pastor Nordtveit carried a lot of influence with me, I have a certain amount of influence with the Bishop. After all, I've been married to him for over 25 years. You should expect your formal letter of approval within a week, and then your name could potentially be placed into nomination for a call any time after that."

"Wow!" was all Michael could say.

"Also," Pastor Sloan concluded, before formally adjourning the meeting, "your name will be put on a list of Supply Pastors. With such a large clergy shortage in our area, you can be kept quite busy preaching in vacant congregations until you receive a permanent call somewhere. And with so many vacant congregations, don't be surprised if that call doesn't come sooner rather than later."

It was all too much for him to take in at once. He sat there as the meeting was adjourned.

"Wow!" he said again, the only coherent word he could muster.

CHAPTER TWENTY THREE

now

Things had been so bad for so long that it didn't seem like they'd ever get any better. Then suddenly the skies seemed to brighten and hope seemed a little more obtainable. That rainbow was out there somewhere, he thought.

Even before leaving the Synod office, he set up a number of supply preaching assignments, including one for Christmas Eve. As soon as he got home, he called Eric and tried as best he could to explain his appreciation for all Eric had done for him. But no words could adequately do the job. But the only thing Eric wanted to know was if Michael's faith had been restored. When Michael explained that it had been and how it came about, that was the only thanks Eric needed. He was happy. Michael could hear it in his voice.

Of course, not everything was perfect. There was still the custody matter to deal with. That was still a major obstacle, and the only thing that really mattered. Still, even here Michael felt the spark of hope. He was able to pray and turn it all over to God. True peace was settling upon him at last.

He turned his thoughts toward Christmas. There were presents to buy. A house to decorate. And a Christmas sermon to prepare.

But all that could wait. The girls would be home from school soon. He couldn't wait to tell them the news. He wasn't sure they would understand it all. But he didn't care. He wanted to share his happiness with them. There hadn't been enough happiness in that house for a long time. As he waited for the bus, he noticed something was missing in the house. Yeah, there were no Christmas decorations yet, but …

"Oh no!" he gasped. They still hadn't gotten a tree! "Great!" he said excitedly. Now he knew what he and the girls would be doing as soon as they got home. This was going to be a joyful Christmas. Once again there was room in his heart to receive the Christ child.

December 23rd. Michael tried to put the finishing touches on his sermon as he waited for the girls to get back from a shopping excursion with their grandparents. It was starting to feel quite normal. Mildred and Gerald had become a part of the family. They were allowed unsupervised visits with the girls, although Anita Bamert still had to approve each visit.

Michael stopped stressing out over each visit. He still worried over how it would all turn out, but he didn't let it consume him. He was learning to take each new day as it came.

The girls came rushing in through the door in their usual way, carrying bags with them. He had gotten used to their always coming home with something given to them by their grandparents.

"We've got presents!" Lisa announced, running up to Michael in the living room. Becky was right behind her with her own bags.

"I see." Michael said. "But you know Christmas is only two days away. Santa Claus will be bringing you presents too. I hope you didn't get too much."

Michael looked over at Mildred and Gerald, standing by the edge of the couch.

"These presents aren't for us." Becky said. "They're for you."

"For me?"

"Yes!" Becky continued. "Grandma and Grandpa helped us."

"But we picked them out ourselves." Lisa emphasized. "We even wrapped them."

"Well that's really nice of you. Shall we put them under the tree?" Michael looked over at Mildred and Gerald. "That was really nice of you too."

As the girls joyfully put their presents under the tree, Michael's attention was focused on the other two adults in the room. They seemed more tentative than usual. Mildred, particularly, looked uncomfortable.

"Is everything all right?" he asked.

"Michael, we have something we want to say to you." Mildred took a step forward, then stopped. She seemed to be struggling to find the right words. "This isn't us. It isn't who we are. This whole lawsuit, it ..."

"I believe what my wife is trying to say is that we believe in God." Gerald stepped in to help his stumbling wife. "We believe in The Golden Rule – 'Do Unto Others as You Would Have Them Do Unto You'. This whole lawsuit thing is not who we are. It's just that we didn't know you, didn't know a thing about you. It was our pastor who suggested we consult an attorney in our congregation. That attorney convinced us we should protect ourselves by being proactive. We went along with him very reluctantly."

"We never wanted to hurt you." Mildred spoke up. "We only wanted to make sure that the girls were all right, that they were in a safe, nurturing environment. And now we know they are. So Michael, we have a gift for you."

"A gift?" Michael was totally bewildered.

"Call it a Christmas present, son." Gerald said. "We're telling our lawyer to drop the whole thing."

"What?" Michael was unsure what he was hearing.

"We want to do this the right way." Gerald continued. "No lawyers. Just good people working things out in an honorable way."

"I'm not sure what to say." Michael was trying hard to take in all that was happening. But it was going too fast for him. The past four months had seemed to drag on forever. Could it all be ending so quickly?

"Now that we've come to know you, we see that you're a good person, Michael. You're an honorable man. You love the girls and they love you. All we ask is that you let us be a part of our granddaughters' lives."

"That's all we've ever wanted, Michael." Mildred's voice sounded almost pleading. "Please allow us that."

"However you want to work it out, son." Gerald put his hand on Michael's right shoulder. "I'm sure we can work it out together, maybe over a nice lunch. What do you say?"

"Yes! I say yes!" Michael couldn't contain the rush of joy at finally realizing the battle was over. He had won.

"Wonderful." Gerald shook Michael's hand.

"Oh thank you. Thank you." Mildred rushed over and hugged Michael.

"Listen." Michael began, after Mildred finally released her hold on him. "Tomorrow I'm leading the Christmas Eve worship service at Trinity Lutheran Church over in Red Bank. It's only a few miles from here. Why don't you come? Then you can sit with the girls while I lead worship. And then on Christmas Day you can come over early and watch the girls open their presents. Then later we can talk over Christmas dinner."

Gerald took a quick glance at Mildred's approving face, then answered, "We'll be there. Thank you, Michael."

"No, thank you." Michael said. "You've made this the best Christmas ever."

"Well, maybe not as good as the first one." Gerald observed. "But it's right up there."

CHAPTER TWENTY FOUR

now

He stood in the pulpit and looked down at his prepared sermon. He had spent hours on it and was quite pleased with the outcome. It was based around the Christmas TV cartoon 'How The Grinch Stole Christmas'. He was quite proud of it. But then he looked out at the congregation, bathed in soft light from the glow of the candles in their holders at the end of each pew. The sanctuary was filled with strange faces, but he could see clearly Becky and Lisa, sitting near the front, looking up at him, sitting between Gerald and Mildred. Seeing the two girls filled him with warmth, as he ignored his prepared text and began speaking from the heart.

"Tonight we gather as a family." he began. "I know that may sound strange. I don't know you and you don't know me. But I look out and I can see families gathered together. I see clearly some mothers and fathers sitting with their children. Others I see sitting together that I'm not quite sure how you're related, but yet I still see family. Some of you may have come alone here tonight. But know that you too are among family. Together, we are the body of Christ and, as such, we are all a part of God's family. Families can come in a variety of combinations, some traditional, some not so traditional. Tonight my own family is here worshipping with you, and while I won't go into detail, suffice it to say that we fall into the non-traditional category. But we are family all the same, and it is our privilege to be here with you to be part of your family tonight."

Michael paused for a moment and looked again at the girls, who were happily drawing with crayons on their bulletins. He smiled, as he continued, "I didn't always appreciate family. But now I have come to see just how important family is to me. It is a special gift. A gift from God. Two thousand years ago God gave us the best gift of all – his son! In Jesus Christ, the Word became flesh. God came to us as a baby, born in a non-traditional way. It's an amazing story. A virgin received in faith the words of an angel. She would conceive and bear a son. Joseph, her fiancé, accepted in faith what an angel told him, and together they traveled to the little town of Bethlehem, where Mary gave birth to her son and named him Jesus. Jesus entered into this world under the most humbling of conditions, born in a manger, a place for the animals. Soon, some shepherds came to visit with a remarkable tale of angels in the sky. Then, following a star, some visitors from the East dropped by bringing presents."

"All these strangers came together because of that one baby and in their own way became a family. God shared His son with Mary and Joseph. They shared the baby with shepherds and Wise Men. God gave us a new definition of family. We are all God's children. That's the message of Christmas. God came to earth and proclaimed 'We're a family!' Before then, people feared God. They saw him as some vengeful judge, standing far removed from His creation. But God wanted to correct that viewpoint. God wasn't a vengeful judge, but a loving parent. God wasn't removed from His creation. In Jesus Christ God became one of us and walked among us, going through the same things we do – joy and pain, love and loss, suffering and even death. And Jesus showed us who God really was. Abba. Father. And Jesus told us that we are all God's beloved children. We are sisters and brothers of Christ himself. We are a family!"

Michael paused, as he felt the moment right to wrap up his thoughts. "So tonight take a moment to look at those around you. They are your sisters and brothers. On this blessed Christmas Eve say a prayer of thanksgiving for this family God has given you. Appreciate them. And try to love them, just as God loves you."

Michael paused again as a closing thought came to him.

"You know, usually I end a sermon by saying 'Amen'. But tonight I'd like to end a different way and ask you to repeat it after me."

He took in a deep breath, then exclaimed loudly, "We are a family!"

And it filled his soul with gladness to hear the entire congregation respond as one, "We are a family!"

EPILOGUE

It was a bright August day. Another school year would be starting in just another week. It was incredible how fast time was going. So much had changed in one year. The biggest change was Michael's new job. Shortly after his approval by the Candidacy Committee, Michael accepted a call to be Pastor of Trinity Lutheran Church, the same church where he had preached his Christmas sermon. And he had that sermon to thank for his new call. The congregation asked the Bishop specifically for him to interview for the position of Pastor. And he readily accepted. It was a nice congregation. The people seemed great. But most importantly, the church was close enough that he didn't need to move and uproot the girls. This made the girls very happy.

Equally delighted were Mildred and Gerald, who purchased the house they had been renting to be close to the girls. Now they were all living in the same town. Even though Mildred could sometimes get on his nerves with her invasive ways, she really was a sweet woman and could be very helpful at times, especially when Michael needed some help with cooking or with raising girls. And she was always happy to babysit when Michael's duties as Pastor demanded his attention or he just needed a little break. Gerald, the man of few words, became a valuable source of wisdom whenever Michael needed some advice. He was also handy with fix-it jobs around the house. Michael called upon him often.

Michael's sister surprised everyone, including her husband Roger, when in February she announced she was expecting another baby. She was due the end of September, but she was still only a phone call away whenever Michael needed someone to talk to.

Miss Piggy and her new friend Cocoa were thriving. And Jedidiah the cat remained as elusive and secretive as ever. But every now and then he appeared at Michael's bedside and settled in for a nap on Michael's legs. Michael let him stay there. Jedidiah's presence made him feel like Jenny was still there.

Still not a day went by without him thinking about Jenny. But the bitterness was gone. Only the fond memories remained. He still missed her. The hole was still there and refused to be filled. But Becky and Lisa were creating new spaces for him. Good spaces. They were such happy little girls. But they were growing so fast. Too fast. He was trying to hold onto each memory, while at the same time living in the moment. Which is what brought them today back to Great Adventure. One last fling before the start of school.

"That was fun." Michael said, as they came off the Pirate Ship ride. "What do you want to do next?"

"Let's do that water ride we did last year." Becky said, excitedly.

"You mean that raft thing?"

"No." Lisa protested. "I didn't like that. It spun around too much."

"I mean that other ride we went on where you got all wet."

"Yeah." Lisa giggled. "You looked funny."

"You really want to go on that again?" Michael asked.

They both piped in, "Yeah!"

"All right. Let's do it."

After a long wait in line, they got on the ride. It seemed to be over in a flash. They got off the boat and started for the exit. Then they came to the same fork in the exit path. Michael started toward the shorter right exit.

"Aren't you gonna go to the wet part?" Lisa asked.

"You want to go and get hit by the wave?" Michael asked, surprised.

"Not us. You." Becky said.

"No, I don't think so."

"Go ahead. We'll wait right by the exit. Promise."

"No, really, it's …" Michael paused. Maybe the little boy in him hadn't completely gone away. "Well …, why not."

He headed toward the walkway where the wave rose to meet the people standing there to greet it. This time he stood against the wall with all the others. It wasn't long before the boat headed down the hill, forcing the spray of water up into the air. Michael kept his eyes open to the last possible second to see the wave approach him. For just a millisecond, he caught a glimpse of something. It wasn't an arc. It wasn't big or up in the sky. But the prism of colors was there as the sun hit off the water.

"Well I'll be …" Michael said softly through his laughter. He was soaking wet once again. But he was loving every second of it. He decided to stick around the walkway for one more splashing. This time, he would keep his eyes open, no matter what – and look for the rainbow.

CPSIA information can be obtained at www.ICGtesting.com
Printed in the USA
BVOW08*1314240615

405992BV00001B/1/P